Cruising for Love

Emily Walters

Cruising for Love

Published by Emily Walters

Copyright © 2019 by Emily Walters

ISBN 978-1-07145-566-1

First printing, 2019

www.EmilyWaltersBooks.com

PRINTED IN THE UNITED STATES OF AMERICA

Dedication

I want to dedicate this book to my beloved husband, who makes every day in my life worthwhile. Thank you for believing in me when nobody else does, giving me encouragement when I need it the most, and loving me simply for being myself.

Table of Contents

Chapter 1

"So how did you do, Margaret? Don't make me wait any longer!"

Margaret Kassmel bit back a smile as she sat her bag on the chair, the excitement of her friend's voice adding another layer to what she was already experiencing. She had looked forward until their shift at Jeff's Café to tell Sharon, wanting to see her reaction in person. After five years of working alongside her, Margaret knew that Sharon couldn't stand to wait for anything. "I gave it my best performance, Sharon. They asked a great deal of questions about my experience."

"Geez, Margaret, quit stalling and just tell me already, will you?" Sharon exclaimed, her hands on her slim hips.

"I got the job! I can't believe it but I got the job! You are looking at the next dance instructor for the cruise ship *Intrepid*."

"That is awesome! I had no doubt of course. When do you leave?"

"In one week. Thank God you told me to get my passport ahead of time. I've already put my vacation time in with Jeff. I can't believe it, Sharon! A bona-fide, stress-free vacation that I don't have to pay for. It's like a dream come true."

Sharon hugged her and gave her a wide smile, the excitement in her eyes mirroring Margaret's. "I am so jealous! I have two left feet but you are a vision when you dance. It's going to be so much fun! Now hurry, we don't have much time before the crowd comes in."

Margaret quickly changed out of her street clothes and donned her waitress uniform, the excitement of what she had experienced still fresh in her mind. She had done it. She, Margaret Kassmel, had beat out a room full of talented dance instructors to grab a spot on the entertainment team on the luxury cruise liner *Intrepid*. She would be the dance instructor for the passengers, taking her passion for teaching to a new level. For ten years she had taught classes of salsa, cha-cha, and ballroom to the community at the local dance studio/community center. Margaret loved the interaction between herself and her students, feeling particularly proud as they succeeded from her tutelage. Now she would do the same, just in a different venue. Not to mention the chance to experience the cruise itself! Her waitressing salary would never allow her the opportunity to enjoy a luxury cruise such as the *Intrepid*. No, most of her money, including the money she made teaching dance, went to paying her bills each month.

Tucking her shirt into her pants, Margaret grabbed her apron and walked out of the tiny back room that served as an employee locker room, the smells of coffee and toast assaulting her senses. "Hey Jeff, what's going on tonight?" she asked, nodding at the owner of Jeff's Cafe. A small business owner, Jeff wore many hats in his own establishment, including that of cook on occasion. Tonight was one of those occasions.

"I hope you girls have your running shoes on tonight. It's been one heck of a day and the night shift ain't looking much better. By the way, congrats on the offer; I really hate to lose you for fourteen days."

"Fifteen if you count the day before I leave," she replied with a laugh. "They will go by before you know it. By the time you actually get around to missing me I will be back."

"Yeah, yeah. Still doesn't help that I am going to be down a waitress for fourteen, no fifteen days."

Margaret stuck out her tongue at him and grabbed a tray ready for the dinner crowd. Though her outward appearance exuded confidence and excitement, inwardly she was nervous and a bit scared at the thought of taking this vacation by herself. While she was super excited about the opportunity, the thought of the unknown gave her butterflies. Waitressing was something she was good at and felt comfortable doing. Dancing was something that she had perfected, honed to a skill that had served her well. When she danced, well, the world melted away. It was her stress relief. Sighing, Margaret tucked a pencil behind her ear and smoothed back her brunette curls. She would enjoy the experience, enjoy the chance at a vacation that she could never afford herself and then come back with a mind full of memories and tons of stories to share.

***

Two hours later, Margaret deposited the plates in the sink and wiped her forehead on her sleeve, her feet aching. Saturday nights were always busy for them and even though the building was small, it was packed to the gills with hungry patrons. She and Sharon had not even had the chance to stop for a break, their tables filling just as fast as they could get them cleaned.

"New customer, table four," Sharon said as she passed, her arms loaded down with dishes. "He's a cutie too."

"Everyone with their own hair and teeth is a cutie to you," Margaret laughed, pushing open the door to the dining room. Sure enough, one lone customer sat at her table, his eyes scanning the menu before him. The café tended to get a lot of businessmen with its proximity to a chain of hotels just a block over, but this one was different. Unlike the rest of their usual customers, his expensive suit put him woefully out of place. Putting on a smile to hide her tiredness, Margaret walked up to the table, pulling out her notepad. "Hi, welcome to Jeff's. What can I get you to drink?"

"Unsweetened tea," he replied, not bothering to look up. "With a plastic spoon, not a metal one."

"Do you know what you would like to eat? We are famous for our burgers and hand- cut fries."

"Heart attack waiting to happen," he grumbled, his deep voice expressing his displeasure with her suggestion. "I would like the grilled chicken, no cheese, no bacon and a side salad, no dressing." He then handed her the menu without looking up, pulling out a sleek cell phone from his suit jacket in the process. Keeping her smile, Margaret wrote down the order and walked away to place it with Jeff. A health nut; she was not surprised. They were getting more and more of those these days. Grabbing the tea and spoon, Margaret walked back to the table.

***

Dominic Graham sighed as he fired off another text to his assistant, reminding her to send the file in the morning. It was one more thing that he had forgotten to do before leaving. George Hamilton, the owner of Hamilton International, would be pissed if he didn't have it to review prior to his meeting with the board. The report contained the last six months of financial acquisitions and having that information was crucial to show that the company was still functioning at the highest capacity. Without it, Hamilton wouldn't have a leg to stand on in terms of the direction of the company for the next three months. The board only met once a quarter for the official review and the members would not like it if they had nothing to discuss. The board members were from all over the world and getting them together in the same room was difficult enough.

As CEO, Dominic was George's right-hand man and presided over many of the company's day-to-day functions. It was a difficult job, but Dominic liked the stress, liked the challenge of winning yet another business transaction. He had grown the company twofold since coming on board eight years ago, rising to become the youngest CEO in the company's history. Dominic was often compared to George himself when he first started the company, ruthless in business and always out to get nothing but the most profitable of transactions, contracts, and acquisitions. There wasn't anything that Dominic couldn't accomplish. "If I didn't know any better, I would think you could be of my own flesh and blood," George had joked often in Dominic's early days at Hamilton International. "I only see you moving up in this company, Dominic."

Receiving the confirmation that she would indeed send the file, Dominic placed his cell phone back in his pocket and sat back. He had only been gone for a couple hours from California but wondered if maybe he was making a mistake with this trip. The business side of it, he could handle and handle pretty quickly. The owner of the small company was to retire from the business world and acquiring this company would open a door to clients that previously had been out of Dominic's reach, clients that hadn't always trusted the big fish in the pond in the past. The deal Dominic had offered him was more than fair. It was the booking of the cruise that he was thinking was a mistake, considering it had been a last-minute decision, something that he didn't normally do. George was not pleased about this sudden "business trip" in the midst of another acquisition that would take the international corporation to the very top.

"This trip cannot be bigger than this deal," George had said angrily when Dominic had informed him of his plans. "Surely you can reschedule until after this transaction and the wedding. That company is just a small fish; we need to reel in the bigger fish, son. Wait until after the wedding. Sunny Florida will be a nice place to take Samantha while you do business."

Dominic's upcoming wedding to Samantha Hamilton, George's only child, had the business world talking. His marriage to the sole heir would solidify Dominic's career future and make him a co-owner of Hamilton International once he became part of the family. While Samantha worked in her father's company currently, she had relayed to him that it wasn't her ambition to continue once they were married. He had latched onto that and never looked back. He wanted to be George, that was without a doubt. There was nothing else he wanted in life but to be at the head of a company, a successful company. It had taken blood, sweat, and tears to work his way up the ladder, ignoring family, friends, and virtually anyone who had stood in his way. He had dated very little, his relationships failing because of his dedication to his career.

Samantha understood Dominic's passion to succeed, after all she was a product of George Hamilton. As a junior executive in her father's marketing department, she was used to the late nights and the constant pressures of the business world. After they were introduced by her father, their relationship blossomed into attraction and mutual respect. He cared for her, liked her, understood her, and it had been only natural that the next step in their two-year relationship would be marriage, making him a part of the Hamilton family.

The wedding was to take place in a month at the exclusive country club that catered to the Hamilton family. He would be just glad to see it done and over with so his life would return to his idea of normal. Since the engagement had been announced, he was the one everyone wanted to see, to meet with, because one day he would be calling all the shots. There was no privacy for him anymore, no chance to take a breath or two before his life took another turn and he was a married man. Everything in the business sense had been accomplished. Everything that he had set out to do was now aligning perfectly with his life and the last step, the most important step if he wanted to continue to move upward, was to get married to Samantha. Their marriage would fulfill his greatest dream of becoming a co-owner of the company.

When the commercial for the luxury cruise had shown on the TV in his penthouse apartment, he had scoffed at the idea. He had no time, there wasn't enough time. Besides, being a CEO meant that he had a great deal of responsibility not only to the company he stood to inherit, but also to himself. Vacations, time off, personal time was not something Dominic ever did.

The second time he had viewed the commercial, though, the thought of being able to refocus without the constant distractions of the upcoming wedding appealed to him greatly. He could use a break from work, enjoy himself as his single days were numbered. The commitment to being a married man in a family such as the Hamilton family would eat up any personal time he used to have. The endless amount of scheduled appearances would double in size and Dominic had already seen his personal calendar fill up with dinners and charity events.

Sighing, Dominic examined his manicured nails, willing the food to hurry. To everyone else, including his fiancée, he was heading to Fort Lauderdale for business; a deal that seemed too good not to investigate further. Dominic had done all the booking himself, down to the hotel room, in an effort to remain off the grid for as long as possible. Fourteen days was a long time to close a business deal, but he had done his best to explain to George that the time was needed

"I think putting a face to the name would make a world of difference in this deal," he had told his boss. "Let me go and smooth it over with them, become their friend. I will come back with this deal wrapped up." In reality he would have it done by the end of the week, just in time to set sail on the cruise ship *Intrepid*.

Shifting to find a comfortable place on the plastic bench, Dominic looked around at the now busy café. It would not normally be his first choice, preferring the quiet ambience of a nice restaurant to the hustle and bustle of this small café. The receptionist at the hotel had suggested it for a quick meal and he was too tired to go anywhere else. His flight had been delayed, pushing his arrival four hours behind schedule. The room he had booked had been the wrong one, with two queens instead of the king-sized bed he had requested. It seemed even his luck was against him taking this trip. Running a hand through his hair,

Dominic looked up, seeing the waitress returning with his tea. He noticed for the first time her plain features, the way her uniform made her seem frumpy. It was her hair that garnered even the least bit of interest, long brunette curls that hung down her back.

"Here you are, one unsweetened tea with a plastic spoon."

Shaking out of his thoughts, Dominic turned his attention back to the waitress, who was sliding the tray onto the table. The sliding motion caused the glass to wobble and before he could react, the coldness of the drink was drenching his lap.

"Oh God, I am so sorry!" she said, as he nearly jumped out of the bench in an effort to clear the ice. "I didn't, I – here's some napkins."

Snatching them out of her hand, he wiped at his crotch area, feeling the liquid seep through his pants and his boxers. This was just what he needed! He was tired, hungry, and now drenched in his unsweetened tea. "Is this how you treat your customers by dumping their drink on them? Good God, woman, you need to learn how to walk."

"I can walk just fine," she snapped, her eyes flashing as she looked at him.

Dominic laughed harshly as he mopped up the rest and dumped the sodden napkins on the table, ignoring her outstretched tray. This nondescript waitress was catching an attitude with him? Well, he was ready to bring it on. "Lady, you couldn't walk your way out of a paper bag."

***

Margaret tried to hold back her anger, years of being a waitress helping her to hone her emotions, but never had she been so insulted so quickly! "It was an accident. I will get you another drink."

"Don't bother," he exclaimed, pushing himself out of the booth to stand in front of her.

Lord he was tall, so tall that the top of her head barely reached his shoulder. Still, she did not shrink away, looking directly at him as she tried to explain again. "Listen, it was an accident. Please sit back down and let me get your food and another tea, on the house."

"You expect me to sit soaking wet in this place another minute?" he shot back, reaching into his pocket. "Keep the change, lady, and learn how to walk properly next time, will you? At this rate your boss will be out of business within the month."

"How dare you!" Margaret fired back, her body quivering with anger. "I can't believe how unbelievably rude you are being at this moment."

"Rude? Lady, you are the queen of rude. I can't believe they let you work here with that attitude."

"Margaret," Jeff's voice penetrated her angry haze, his tone telling her to let it go.

"Fine, have a nice day, sir. Thanks for ruining my great afternoon."

"Thanks for ruining the start of my vacation," the man grumbled, walking toward the door.

Her face aflame, she watched as he walked out before turning around, seeing both Sharon and Jeff staring at her. "What? He started it."

"Actually you did by dousing him with tea," Jeff replied with a roll of his shoulders. "It's over and done with, get back to work."

"That man is a bad day walking," Margaret replied, reaching for a rag to wipe the table down. Really, it had only been some spilled tea. It wasn't like she had dumped a whole plate of food on him. Plus she hadn't done it on purpose and had apologized accordingly. It was because of times like this that she would gladly prop her feet up and enjoy herself on her cruise.

Chapter 2

One week later

"Here is your room, Ms. Kassmel. I understand that you are going to be part of our entertainment team for this stretch?"

"I am to be the dance instructor, Bernard," Margaret smiled, reading the man's name tag. "And I couldn't be more excited."

"Well, delightful to have you of course," Bernard replied, opening the door with her room key card. "I will be your personal cabin steward for the next two weeks. Your luggage has already been placed in your cabin."

"Wow," Margaret said as she stepped into the room. This cabin was even bigger and nicer than she expected. Her room was equipped with a queen-sized bed and small couch facing a mounted flat-screen TV. An open closet to her left was filled with her garment bags and suitcases, while the spacious bathroom was off to her right. What was the most impressive were the sliding glass doors at the back of the room, leading to a small balcony that currently was overlooking the port. It was much more impressive than the windowless cabin she had expected. There was no doubt that she was going to be treated as a passenger.

"Enjoy the embarking and your first night on the cruise."

"Thank you, Bernard," she said as he handed her the key card and closed the door, leaving her alone in the space. Spying the bottle of champagne in the chiller, Margaret wasted no time pouring herself a glass and taking a sip, wrinkling her nose as the bubbles tickled it. The last time she had imbibed in champagne was at her cousin's wedding two years ago. This one was mildly sweet, sliding down her throat smoothly. Smiling, Margaret couldn't help but twirl in a circle like a little girl, her heart giddy with excitement. She hadn't expected the five-star treatment, but from the embarking process to the personal steward to this cabin, she felt like royalty. Having the dancing instructor opportunity had been exciting enough, but getting this type of treatment made her really look forward to this vacation. The rest of the ship had to be just as lovely and Margaret couldn't wait to see all of the areas she would hold her classes in.

Walking to the balcony, she threw open the door and stepped out, inhaling the salty air with vigor. All of the worry, all of the nervousness was vanishing rapidly now that she was on board, ready for her adventure. Her duties did not officially start until tomorrow, leaving her the rest of the afternoon and tonight to explore a bit, enjoy what was to be her home for the next two weeks. A horn sounded from somewhere within the ship and Margaret walked back into her room, downing her champagne in one gulp. She would go up to the top deck and wave her current life goodbye for at least two weeks. Nothing could wipe this smile off of her face, nothing at all.

***

"Welcome to your cabin, Mr. Graham. I hope this will suffice for your stay."

Dominic grunted as he moved into the spacious cabin, squinting against the brightness of the sun flooding the room. At least it was bigger than his hotel room, with a large sitting area that led to the balcony, the view that of nothing but blue ocean as far as he could see. To his left, he could see the bedroom, the view of the ocean continuing along the wall.

"I am James, your steward for the length of your stay. As you can see, your luggage has already arrived. You will find the whiskey you requested on the bar to your right. Ice is located in the mini fridge. Is there anything else you require?"

"No," Dominic sighed, glad that his vacation was starting off on the right foot. After a week of attempting to close the business deal, he had finally succeeded in getting the owner to agree to his terms, therefore making the deal final just hours before he was to be on this boat.

"Please let me know if you need anything else. Enjoy your evening."

Dominic just nodded as the steward closed the door, removing both his jacket and tie as he crossed the room to the bar. A good stiff drink was in order to start this vacation right, to clear his mind of the entire past week and prepare for two weeks of whatever he cared to do. The fiery liquid burned as he chased the first one down, appreciating that the steward had indeed gotten the brand correct. A pamphlet lay next to the bottle on the bar, showcasing all that the cruise would offer in terms of entertainment on board. There were classes galore, from dancing to cooking. There were high-stakes poker tournaments, Broadway shows, and lectures. The spa services were extensive, from in-room massages to all-day affairs in the ship's world-class spa. He planned to take full advantage.

With a sigh, Dominic walked to the balcony just as the horn sounded, settling into the plush lounge chair overlooking the endless ocean. While he would enjoy what was offered on board, most of his time would be spent sitting in this chair, planning his future. He intended to come back refreshed, revitalized, and with so many directions that the company could go in that George's head would spin. He wanted to show him that he was ready to take on the added responsibilities, to move the company into the right direction for the future. Propping up his feet on the railing, Dominic closed his eyes against the sun and stretched his arms over his head. Dinner was a long ways off so he might as well catch up on a well-deserved nap. He hadn't slept very well in the hotel the last few days and he felt exhausted.

Chapter 3

Margaret turned this way and that in front of the mirror, looking at her dress with a critical eye. It was a classic little black dress, showing off her toned arms and just a hint of thigh peeking through the small slit in the front. She paired it with red heels that matched her clutch, hoping that she looked sophisticated enough to mingle with the passengers. After the ship had pulled away from port she had stayed topside for a while, enjoying the salty air in her hair and sun on her skin while she watched the passengers that she would be coming in contact with. Most were couples, a variety of ages that had her excited to think how she could tailor the classes around what age group showed up. Some people liked high-intensity dancing, the faster the better, while others enjoyed the closeness that some of the older dances, like ballroom, brought between the couple. Margaret did not have a favorite, she loved them all.

Flipping her hair over her shoulder, Margaret decided that her clothing was adequate enough and left her room, following the passageway to the grand staircase. She was fortunate enough be on the same floor as the posh atrium of the *Intrepid*, its gleaming interior softly lit for the night. Soft piano music from the polished baby grand piano drifted through the air as well-dressed passengers made their way to dinner, many of them in full evening attire. Margaret tried not to stare as they floated past, the diamonds in their ears and around their necks twinkling in the soft light. It was no doubt that this was a true luxury cruise and Margaret couldn't help but feel a bit out of place amid the glitz and glamour. Squaring her shoulders, she forced a confident smile on her face as she followed the group, knowing that wealth did not make the person.

Margaret found her table and took a seat, placing her evening clutch in her lap. She was the first one at her table and it gave her enough time to gather her thoughts and to actually start looking forward to the meal she would enjoy tonight. It wasn't long before the other chairs started to fill up with three couples, leaving just one other chair to her right empty. At least she wouldn't be the only single person among all of these other couples. The awkwardness of the introductions was quickly done and the table lapsed into silence once more as they awaited the waiter. Margaret chose to pick up her menu and nearly salivated over the choices. Lobster, filet mignon, mahimahi, the choices were endless. The chair next to her scraped against the wood flooring as the final party of the table arrived, settling in next to her. She took in his scent first, a spicy smell that reminded her of oranges and cedarwood. Glancing over, she took in his dark grey pants and crisp white shirt, glad to see that he wasn't wearing a tux like the rest of the men at the table. Putting on a smile, she lowered the menu and turned toward him, extending her hand.

"Looks like we are to be table mates." As he turned, her smile melted into a frown, her eyes narrowing as she recognized him. Of all the rotten luck! "You?"

***

Dominic heard the question in her voice as he laid eyes on her, taking in the glossy hair that fell in soft curls on her tanned shoulders, her black dress tight but demure at the same time. Her wide blue eyes were displaying shock rather than the kindness her voice had expressed just a moment before and it didn't take long for his brain to register why. It was the waitress from the café he visited over a week ago, but what the heck had happened to her? Gone was the frumpy, angry brunette and in her place was this woman, a beautiful woman that no doubt turned many a head in that dress tonight. What he didn't like was the angry darts she was shooting at him at the moment. Granted, she had seen him at his worst a week ago, tired and frustrated on how his trip was starting out. The hotel was located next to a construction site that seemed to be working on the night shift, the sounds of beeping equipment keeping him up most of the nights he was there. It didn't help that the hotel was booked solid, throwing out his idea of changing rooms. He had unfairly taken it out on her and her simple mistake of spilled tea. She had just been a stranger that had pushed him over the edge.

Dominic hadn't ever been one to make apologies but since she was sitting next to him, he had the perfect opportunity to make amends, especially since they were on the same ship in the middle of the ocean.

"Listen, I –" She didn't give him a chance to go any further.

"Tell me this is not happening." Pushing away from the table, she walked away, her long hair swaying angrily with each step.

With a frustrated oath, Dominic also left the table, following her out of the dining room and into the passageway, ignoring the looks around him. "Wait, please." She stopped then, her shoulders lifting in what must have been a large breath before she turned to face him, anger and a bit of hurt radiating from her.

"Listen, I don't care to hear what you have to say. God, I can't believe it, this has to be the worst joke ever played by fate."

Dominic inwardly winced at her biting words, surprised that she was here as well. How on God's green earth had a waitress been able to afford this type of cruise? The amount of money he had forked out had been astronomical even to his bank account. "I just want to apologize for my behavior last week."

"You were one of the absolute worst customers I have ever had. You embarrassed me for no reason over an accident," she shot back, pointing a red-tipped finger at him in the process. Gone was the polite waitress and in her place was this fiery vixen that was surprising the hell out of him.

"I – I'm sorry," he stammered, idly wondering how she would stand against a room full of competitors. One look from her and he was blubbering an apology immediately. He didn't apologize to anyone.

"I, grrr, just leave me alone. I don't accept your apology," she finally said, turning away. "Just stay away from me." She then walked away, her anger radiating in her stride.

Dominic swallowed hard, fighting the urge to go after her. God she was gorgeous. He would have never guessed that under that waitress outfit she was hiding a killer body.

"Flowers, honey," an elderly woman said as she passed by him, patting him on the arm like a grandmother would. "A lot of flowers will make her forgive you."

Dominic laughed and rubbed a hand over his face, surprised at how shaken he was from their encounter. "Ma'am, I don't think flowers will work on this one."

Chapter 4

"And now one, two, three. Mr. Grey, remember to hold your elbow up. Mrs. Grey, eyes on your husband. Let the steps come naturally."

Margaret smiled as she watched the elderly couple attempt the cha-cha on the dance floor, wishing all the people she had instructed were as cute as this couple. She had woken with a renewed energy this morning, excited about her first day as dance instructor. After finding the entertainment director, she was placed in one of the many nightclubs on board, complete with a wood dance floor. Latin music pounded from the speakers, its sultry rhythm having all of the dancers tapping their toes along with the music. It was one of Margaret's favorite dances; the moves, the interaction with one's partner. She could dance it all night.

Her first dance lesson had a better turnout than she had expected, with eleven couples currently fumbling their way through the cha-cha. Her classes would be two hours a day, enough time to teach the attendees two simple dances. Thankfully they were in the morning, which allowed Margaret to enjoy the rest of the afternoon however she pleased. It was a dream come true, a job she was especially excited to be part of. Well, other than her surprise at dinner last night.

How on earth could it possibly have happened that she would be on the same cruise ship as he was? Not only the same cruise, but also the same table? What was going to be next, sharing the same cabin? The thought of running into him constantly made her want to grind her teeth. He was rude, inconsiderate and in need of some serious anger management classes. She could only hope that on the cruise his attitude would improve or the crew was in for a hard time with him.

Remembering that she was in the presence of customers, Margaret forced her attention back to her class. She would not let him ruin this opportunity to have a great time on this cruise. She would not let him ruin her vacation either. She would avoid him at all costs and hope to the heavens above that he would do the same.

***

Dominic placed his sunglasses in his pocket as he walked through the passageway, feeling drawn to the sound of pulsating music. He had awakened in a pretty decent mood, hitting the gym before half of the ship was even awake. A creature of habit, Dominic always awoke at 5 a.m. back home to hit the gym, always feeling alert and refreshed after having done so. Dominic then showered and instead of changing into his customary full suit, he opted for a pair of khaki shorts and T-shirt. Later he hoped to take a swim in the pool on the top deck before choosing what his evening entertainment might be. It was now after ten in the morning and he found himself wandering around the ship, familiarizing himself with what was to be his home for the next thirteen days. Reaching the source of the music, Dominic found himself in the midst of a dance lesson, the couples butchering the cha-cha on the dance floor. Dancing was not something Dominic could say that he had mastered in his lifetime and he couldn't say he actually enjoyed doing it.

"Wonderful! You are all doing just lovely! Just keep it up and you will be masters in no time." That voice.

Stepping just inside the doorway, Dominic leaned against the wall as he watched her in the midst of the dance floor, a wide smile on her face. Today she had her hair pulled up into an elegant bun, her uniform consisting of a sleeveless white shirt and knee- length skirt that moved easily with her movements. Her face was flushed with exertion and as she turned in his direction, he saw that she wore a name tag on her shirt. How interesting. First she was a waitress in that café and now she was an instructor on a cruise ship? He was intrigued, very intrigued.

Being as quiet as possible, he quickly understood that dancing was her element, much like business was his. She fairly glowed as she gave small instructions to each of her couples, making sure she talked with all of them, giving them the feeling that she was personally catering to them. He had to admire that, for it was a trick that he used in the business world. Find the one thing that a potential customer enjoyed, whether it be their family, fishing, spending money... and hone in on that hobby. It gave him a leg up on any competitor and gave the customer a false sense of caring. He doubted that it was the same for her. He watched as she moved to the DJ booth and switched the music to a soft orchestra style, clapping her hands to get their attention.

"Time to practice our waltz from earlier. Mr. and Mrs. Grey, will you lead us?" An elderly couple gave her quick nods as they assumed the waltz position, moving slowly across the floor to the music.

He could see that, did her name tag say Margaret? She didn't look like a Margaret. He would have thought her a Rachel or Julia. Margaret sounded so old-fashioned and there was nothing about her that was old-fashioned. Good God, her legs went on forever under that skirt! Shaking out of his thoughts, Dominic ran a hand over his face, surprised at himself. Why was this woman under his skin so badly? She was just a waitress that he had experienced one, no two, run-ins with. Why did he care to apologize to her so much? He should just let it go and enjoy himself on this vacation.

Pushing himself off the wall, Dominic took one last look at Margaret, her eyes shining as she watched her pupils fumble around the dance floor. He needed to forget her, forget that he even owed her the slightest apology. She was a distraction that he didn't need if he was to enjoy this cruise. Besides, the way she had responded to him last night wasn't a good indication that they would enjoy each other's company.

Chapter 5

Margaret stepped into the lively bar, smiling at the atmosphere. She had decided she deserved something special to top off what had been a great start to this vacation. Her class had gone swimmingly and the afternoon by the pool had been full of bright sun and a good steamy romance novel that had kept her occupied for hours. She felt better than she had in months and after eating dinner in one of the other dining rooms, Margaret hadn't wanted the night to end. Wearing a white strapless dress that showed off her amazing tan, she smiled at the approaching bartender. "A glass of white wine, please."

"Coming right up," he grinned, turning away with a wink.

Settling into the chair, Margaret set her clutch on the bar and looked around, noticing that the place was fairly packed. Music pulsated out of the speakers above, the floor busy with dancers of all ages moving to the beat. Couches and chairs were situated on the outer edges, passengers congregating with friends, laughter intermingling with the music. This was definitely what she needed, somewhere to unwind and let go for just a little while. The bartender returned with her wine and she gave him a smile as she tasted it. It was fruity with a hint of sweetness as it glided over her tongue, her taste buds bursting at the flavor.

Spinning around, she faced the dance floor, watching the dancers before her. Dancing was a way to let go, to enjoy yourself whether or not you could actually dance. She had enjoyed it for many years, the way she felt when she moved to the music. All her stress and issues would melt away and Margaret would lose herself in the moves. She wanted to pass on that to each person she taught dance to, to enjoy that freedom if only for a dance or two.

"Why aren't you out there? They could stand a dance lesson or two." Whirling around, Margaret collided with a pair of cool blue eyes, the smell of spicy orange cologne assaulting her senses.

"Why are you here?" Up close he was unbelievably handsome with a chiseled jaw showing just a hint of dark stubble dusting the surface. His hair was medium brown and haphazard about his head, as if he ran his fingers through it constantly, a lock falling boyishly on his wide forehead. It was those eyes that were most intriguing. Who was he? Why was he here, alone? What was his story and why was he seeking her out?

"That's a loaded question," he said softly near her ear, his voice causing her to shiver involuntarily. "Do you mean on this boat or next to you?"

"Either, neither. I thought I told you to stay away from me," she shot back, her fingers gripping her glass tightly. "Wait a minute, what did you just say about dancing?"

"Lessons," he started, propping himself against the bar. "I saw your headshot on the itinerary today. So you are a waitress and a dance instructor. What other talents do you have, Margaret?"

"I don't want to talk with you," she said haughtily, though her resolve was starting to weaken somewhat.

He sighed next to her and she fought the smile on her lips, glad to know that she was being somewhat infuriating to him. "I didn't see you at dinner."

"I ate dinner elsewhere. I didn't like the table assignment."

"Don't worry; I ate your portion and mine."

She laughed then, unable to help it. He smiled and her breath caught, wondering how it was possible that the sparkle in his eyes could make him even more handsome.

***

Dominic smiled, her laughter touching somewhere deep inside him, supremely satisfied that he was causing the glow on her face now. He had no earthly idea why his mind would not erase her, would not move on from the mere presence of her face, but it was haunting him. Earlier at dinner he was disappointed to not see her in the seat next to him and it had been by chance that he had seen her walk into this club, his feet forcing him to follow her. He felt like a stalker but his efforts had paid off. She was willing to forgive him for his debacle in the café. He should tell her good night and get back to his room, to work with a clear conscience. But for some reason he was rooted at her side, now intrigued to hear her story, to see if he could coax another laugh out of her. "Now I can sleep at night," he said jokingly. "So back to your talents."

"You are persistent," she smiled, looking back at the dance floor, the dim lighting highlighting her profile. Up close he could see the fine features of her face, the pout of her lips that were devoid of any lipstick. Her hair was down again, falling in soft waves around her face and bare shoulders, the faint smell of flowers drifting into his nostrils. The white dress accentuated her figure that he now knew was honed from dancing, showing off her slim waist and those long legs that stretched forever. He was surprised that she hadn't been approached by anyone but him, her confidence and looks making her nearly impossible to overlook. "I am a waitress, yes, and I do not go around spilling things on my customers on a normal basis. I also teach dancing on the side."

"It's your passion," he interjected, seeing how her features softened at the mention. He could understand. Business, making deals was his passion though a strange one to most. He wanted to succeed at every single one of them, with failure not being an option in his world. That drive had been the reason he was in the position of CEO today, the reason that he would become owner one day.

"Yes it is," she said, taking a deep breath. "I hope to one day leave the waitressing world behind and open my own dance studio."

"A worthy investment," Dominic replied, admiring that she had a plan for her future.

She then turned to him, laughter dancing in her eyes. "Forgive me, here I am telling you all of my plans and do not even know your name. Margaret Kassmel, waitress and dance instructor."

"Dominic Graham, business investor and horrible dancer," he replied, taking her outstretched hand. "A pleasure." Her small hand shook his firmly and he lingered over her soft skin, feeling the first frisson of desire sweep through him. He was attracted to her, that was without a doubt. She was beautiful, confident, and had a drive to succeed.

Margaret laughed again, showing a mouthful of even teeth as she withdrew her hand, wrapping it around the wine glass. "Well, that is unfortunate. Perhaps you just need a good instructor?"

"Perhaps. Do you know of a good one that is around?"

***

Oh my, Margaret thought as the temperature around them notched up a few degrees. She would imagine that he was ruthless as a businessman, those blue eyes turning icy as he pounded out deal after deal. He seemed confident and driven, very sure of who he was, and appeared to be unshaken by anything. "I do know of someone," she said slowly, knowing she was stepping head-first into the fire. "But you will have to listen."

"I can do that," he said softly, his eyes crinkling.

Margaret placed her glass on the bar and held out her hand, accepting the challenge. "Come on then." Hang it all. She was here to have fun and she would start with him. With a slow smile he took her hand and she led him to the dance floor just as the tempo slowed. "The key to dancing is to pay attention to your partner," she started, hoping her voice was not shaking like her knees were. Placing her hands lightly on his arms to position him, she felt a jolt of awareness at his closeness. "And move in the same direction." Shifting her hips, she started a slow, rhythmic sway, urging him close.

He stepped closer and Margaret nearly fumbled in her own steps as his hands settled at her waist, the heat of him searing through her dress. Either he was a quick learner or he had all-out lied about his ability, she thought as she watched him move with her, his body in sync with hers in surprising sureness. His eyes held hers as she moved her hands up to his shoulders, taking in the width of them under his dress shirt. A small patch of tanned skin peeked out from his unbuttoned collar, the sprinkling of dark hair tempting her with every movement. Another couple pushed against him and he stepped even closer, their bodies brushing each other as the music flowed over them. "You lied," she panted.

"I just had a good teacher," he shrugged, his fingers caressing her side.

The music stopped and Margaret stepped back, her heart racing uncontrollably. This was unexpected to say the least. "I – I think I need to turn in for the night." She had to put some distance between them, to clear her mind. This man was dangerous to her. He didn't resist, only followed her off the dance floor to where her forgotten clutch still lay on the bar. Grateful, she accepted it and turned around, flustered to find him so close.

"May I see you again?" he asked. "All dancing aside of course."

"I, uh –" She should say no and walk away. This was not why she was on this vacation, this was not in her plans. Being on a cruise ship and being home accepting a date were two different things. The dance had been fun, a moment of impulse, but it was not meant to lead into more time spent with him, wasn't it?

"Your choice," he continued, his fingers drifting past her cheek to tuck her hair behind her ear. "Anything you wish to do. Just give me a chance to show you that I am not the guy from the café."

"Meet me on top deck after lunch tomorrow," she said hastily, stepping away from his touch. This was a mistake, she could feel it in her bones but the thought of saying no hurt her even more.

Chapter 6

Dominic looked at his wardrobe with care, settling on a pair of swim trunks that could easily pass as shorts and a blue polo shirt that would be acceptable for anything else. He had no idea what their date was going to consist of, but the last thing he wanted to do was have to swim in khakis. He didn't understand it, but he was anticipating the outing with Margaret with more excitement than he probably should have. Their conversation and dance last night had him feeling unlike himself, the business side of him overtaken by a shaken man unsure of himself for the first time in a long time.

"Snap out of it, Dom," he muttered to himself as he pulled on his clothes, running his hands through his hair. She was just going to be someone whose company he happened to enjoy, someone that he could pass the time with. So why had he all but begged to have her meet him today? The thought of their chemistry ending with that dance last night had perturbed him. He wanted more time with her.

Grabbing his key card and sunglasses, Dominic slid his feet into his topsiders and left the room. Another day with her would satisfy his curiosity, he decided. He wanted to know how she came about being on this ship and what was it about her that drew him to her like a moth to the light. An elevator ride later, he arrived topside, the sun hitting him full force. It was another gorgeous day at sea, the pool crowded with sunbathers both in and around the deck. She was waiting for him near the first bar, dressed in a strappy tank top and shorts, a smile on her face. Dominic let out the breath he hadn't known he was holding and approached her, an easy smile on his face. "Good afternoon."

"Good afternoon to you as well," she said, pulling her sunglasses to the top of her head. "Are you ready for some fun?"

"Fun?" he asked. He hadn't known what to expect from her and she wasn't helping out the situation.

With a grin, she pulled out the daily newsletter identical to the one he had received this morning from her pocket. "I haven't been able to do any of the things on board yet so I thought it would be fun to try out some of them. Are you game?"

"I – yes, I am game," he said slowly, wondering which ones she had in mind. If it had anything to do with shopping, like the expensive shops he had noticed near the dining room, or a lecture, he would take a mysterious trip to the bathroom and never return.

"Don't look so scared," she laughed, grabbing his hand. "I won't be mean, I promise. Come on, let's have some fun."

***

Three hours later Margaret grinned as she laid down her cards. "Ha, two pair, aces high."

Across from her, Dominic's smile was slow and sure as he laid down his cards in triumph, the entire table clapping to her dismay. "Full house, darling."

"Great job, you two," the card instructor clapped, before turning to address the other passengers that had participated in the demonstration. "Thank you all for taking part in our little demonstration. Don't be afraid to enjoy the tournaments offered nightly."

"I can't believe you beat me again," she fussed as they left the table. "I did everything the instructor said about bluffing."

Dominic laughed beside her and she punched his arm, feeling particularly upset. She didn't like to lose. "Your eyes," he said, pretending to hold the arm she had hit, a wounded look on his face. "Your eyes light up when you get a good hand."

"My eyes," she grumbled as they walked out into the passageway. "I guess I will have to work on that."

"What's next?" Dominic opened the wrinkled booklet and Margaret couldn't help but stand on her tiptoes to look over his shoulder, taking in his intoxicating smell that she was getting used to. It had been a great afternoon. She had dragged him to cooking classes, where they had learned to chop vegetables with fine precision. From there he had practiced his golf swing and she had taken her chances with the golf club for the first time. The poker session had been Margaret's latest attempt to try something new.

Though he had looked scared to death at first, Margaret had seen the ease settle in Dominic with each lesson, as he found out that she wasn't going to torture him with things like shopping or napkin folding that had been listed in the booklet. No, each lesson was really something she had wanted to experience since she had the chance to and she was very pleased that he had gone along without a word of complaint. She had quickly learned that she was correct in thinking Dominic was ruthless because he hadn't been happy until he had perfected his skill in each lesson they took, even arguing with the cooking instructor who had told him that his vegetables were not up to snuff. She had to nearly drag him out of there.

"Well, the next thing is relatively easy," he was saying, looking at the paper.

"Well, what is it? Wine tasting? I'm pretty good at tasting wine."

He chuckled and looked at her, handing her the paper. "It says you are to have dinner with me in an hour."

"Wow, I didn't realize how fast the afternoon flew by," she stated, looking at her watch. "I can meet you in the dining room."

His fingers reached out and caressed her chin, causing her to look up at him in surprise. It was the first time he had really touched her since the night before and the same spark of heat ignited her body, her breath becoming suddenly shallow. "Not the dining room, Margaret. I want to take you to dinner, just the two of us."

"The two of us?" she stammered, her heart pounding in her ears. That was intimate, personal, and she honestly didn't know if she minded so much the thought.

"I won't bite, Margaret," he continued, dropping his hand from her chin. "Come on, I let you lead today. Let me lead tonight, just for a little while."

Looking into his eyes, she saw the earnestness there and felt her heart melt just a little. He wanted to spend time with her. What was so bad about that? They were both single people on a cruise, looking for some fun in their lives. Once the trip was over, they would depart to their separate lives and she would have this memory for a lifetime. Wasn't this one of those vacation flings Sharon had told her to have, to enjoy herself?

"Okay," she finally said against her better judgment. Dinner still could be innocent enough and if she wanted to throw caution to the wind, then she could do that too.

Chapter 7

"So tell me something about yourself."

Dominic paused midair with his fork, chewing his salad slowly as he looked at his dinner companion. She was a vision tonight, her soft pink wrap dress illuminating her tanned skin, her long hair braided to one side. He had been lost for words when she had arrived at their meeting place, grinning like an idiot as he had taken her hand. He had picked one of the best restaurants on the ship per his steward and so far, the man had been correct. Not only was the restaurant a complete surprise, the way he was acting and feeling was a surprise as well. He hadn't felt so light or worry-free in years. Realizing that she was looking at him expectantly, he laid down his fork and took a sip of his wine. "My life is not that exciting."

"I don't care," she replied, giving him an encouraging smile. "Come on, anything. You know I am a dancer and a waitress from Florida. I don't even know where you are from."

"California. I am a CEO of a large corporation in California."

"The head honcho, how impressive. What else? What do you like to do?"

"I like to work," Dominic said, noticing how hollow the words sounded in his ears. Was that all he really liked to do? "I have very important obligations at work. I don't have much time for anything else."

"That has to be the most boring answer I have ever heard," Margaret said, wrinkling her nose. "You, Dominic Graham, need to find a hobby. Work is not a hobby. Work pays the bills."

Dominic just looked at her, his mind going in a million different directions. What would he do if he didn't have his job? What would be his passion? There was nothing now that really captured his attention, that he enjoyed on a daily basis other than the gym and he really didn't like to do that. He did it because he had done it for years and it was his routine.

"Let's see, a hobby for Dominic. You are pretty good at golf and poker, though I would think losing money wouldn't be that fun."

"I wouldn't lose," he interrupted. "You, on the other hand, would be broke."

"I resent that comment, sir," she laughed, tapping her finger against her cheek. "I would eventually get the hang of winning money instead of losing it. However I would fear for the chef's very life to have you chopping vegetables."

"I did not do anything but show him how wrong he was," Dominic grumbled, looking down at his steak. She had a point though. His life did sound, well, rather boring even to him. Work was his life and he had always had no problem with it, but explaining it to someone else made him sound hollow and uninspiring.

"Don't worry so much about it," she was saying, patting his hand across the table. "I understand your drive and it's fine. A hobby can come later."

It was on the tip of his tongue to ask her to be his hobby, to find something else in him other than the work monster he had become over the years. She was rapidly becoming the light that his life had been missing and a lifetime with her, well, it would never be boring. Instead he cleared his throat and gave her a grin, nodding to her food. "Eat before it gets cold. We would hate to disappoint the chef by returning these plates."

***

Margaret took in a deep breath and smiled, enjoying the cool night air on her face. After a lovely dinner Dominic suggested a stroll on the top deck, the warm night air a perfect end to another perfect day at sea. Now they walked along the wooden deck, the stars out in full force over the dark ocean. She had her hand tucked into the crook of his arm, enjoying his closeness. She had told him more about herself during dinner, how she had come to be on this ship with him. They had laughed over some of their antics from earlier today and she hated for it to come to an end.

"Do you believe in fate?" she asked softly, stopping to look at him. "I mean, do you believe that two people come together for a reason?"

Dominic didn't answer immediately, his large hand coming up to cup her cheek, caressing it with the pad of his thumb. She closed her eyes against his warmth, bringing her hand up to place over his. "I don't know if I believe in fate or luck. The science behind it is not based in truth."

She laughed and opened her eyes, taking her other hand to trace the width of his shoulders with her fingertips. "I should have known you would answer like that."

He gave her a half smile, stepping closer to her with determination in his eyes. She should have been intimidated but instead waited with bated breath on his next move. "I'm going to kiss you, Margaret," he said softly, bringing his other hand up to frame her face.

She couldn't say anything but gave a short nod before his lips descended upon hers. His kiss was soft, the mere brushing of his lips against hers, a shiver of heat descending upon her with every stroke.

She brought her other hand around his neck and he deepened his kiss, nibbling and tasting until she moaned low in her throat. It was intoxicating, his kiss, each sweep of his lips making her want more.

Dominic growled softly before his tongue swept in and Margaret was lost, his taste consuming her. "Margaret," he whispered, rubbing his lips over hers.

"Dear God," she echoed, her knees shaking. She had experienced her fair share of kisses in her lifetime but none had shaken her like this one, none had affected her as deeply as this kiss from the man before her. He captured her lips again and she allowed it, not wanting to let him go. Her fingers were into his hair, her body against his in this tortured dance and sending her thoughts scattering in all directions. Finally, they both came up for air, her leaning into him for support, his arms encircling her waist and holding her close. "That was madness," she whispered, hearing his thundering heartbeat against her cheek. He said nothing but she felt the slightest pressure shift in his arms, cradling her against him. She knew this would be much more than a memory for her. This could be heartbreak.

***

Dominic stalked into his room, slamming the door shut before he moved to the bar, pouring a drink in rapid succession. His hand shook and he forced himself to calm down, leaning against the bar with his hands. He was on fire and it was because of her, because of the innocence of a kiss that he hadn't been able to stop. Now not only was she in his mind, but she was on his lips, the taste of her burning through his very soul as his body demanded more. A simple friendship was turning into so much more and he was very much uncertain. He was stepping into uncharted territory, feeling sensations that he hadn't ever felt with Samantha. It made him feel vulnerable, a feeling he was not used to.

"Argghh!" he yelled, venting his frustrations. Margaret was someone that he could easily crush without meaning to, after all, he had the conquer-and-discard mentality. A piece of him was selfish, wanting to spend more and more time with her to suffice his own need to be near her. A small piece of him knew what he was doing was wrong and he should confess to her now before it went too far, before she got designs on him that he would not be able to fulfill. Margaret was like a rare flower, each petal revealing a part of her that he longed to cherish. It was totally unlike him to be thinking of her as so. This was why his and Samantha's relationship was based on mutual respect and understanding. Love made a man weak, love made a person not concentrate on tangible things, like money and ladder climbing. His relationship with Samantha took all of the tender feelings out of the picture, allowing both of them to stay unaffected by love. Love? Was he really considering himself in love with Margaret?

"You've really lost it now, Dom," he said to himself, thrusting his hand through his hair. He had known her all of what, three days not counting the café? To fall in love that quick, that was unheard of. Wasn't it?

Chapter 8

Margaret hummed softly as she watched her class master the tango, the goofy smile on her face hard to erase this morning. Her dreams had been filled with her blue-eyed CEO, reliving their kiss, and what could have happened that had her blushing as she awoke. Dominic had escorted her back to her room with another lingering kiss and she had been tempted to invite him in, to allow his hands to do more than cradle her hips but at the last moment lost the nerve. She felt like a giddy sixteen-year-old with her first crush but she didn't care. Dominic was definitely the type of man to crush over. What was she so afraid of? It was obvious he wasn't married for she saw no ring or ring line breaking the tan on his finger. He was interested in her, as she was in him. She had shown him fun in his pretty boring life and he at least acted like he enjoyed it. She should be deliriously happy. It was her warning light in the back of her mind that said to slow down, to protect her heart but Margaret feared she was too late in that regard.

"Alright, that's all for today," she finally said, grabbing the attention of her dancers. "You all did superbly. Please come back tomorrow to learn the salsa." As the class filed out, Margaret cut off the music and turned toward the door, her body jolting in awareness of him. Dominic stood just inside the doorway, dressed in his customary polo shirt and khaki shorts she was identifying as his cruising wardrobe. His eyes were on her, his lips curling into his familiar grin that made her heart skip a beat in response.

"Hi."

"All done?" he asked, walking toward her.

"All done for the day."

"Good," he said, sliding his hands along her jaw before he captured her lips with his. Margaret nearly whimpered in response as she realized how much she had missed him and his touch, clinging to his shoulders as he took his fill of her. "I'm glad to see you."

"Me too," she admitted, resting her forehead against his. "This is madness."

"Complete and utter madness," he echoed, dropping his hands to capture one of hers.

"Come on, let's get out of here."

"Where are we going?" she asked as she followed him out of the club and down the passageway.

"Don't you know?" he replied. "We've arrived in the Bahamas."

***

"Oh my God. Do you see how blue that water is? I never would have imagined it to be so blue!"

Dominic chuckled as he watched Margaret experience the crystal-clear waters of the Bahamas, feeling some of her excitement touch him. She had been nearly ecstatic that they had arrived at the first stop of the cruise and after stopping by her room to change, she was the one dragging him down the plank and onto land with the intent of seeing everything. When he had first booked this trip, there was no part of him that wanted to get off at the ports of call. That was before Margaret. Now he sat beside her on the boat, watching her excitement as they cruised about the island, ignoring the tour guide as he droned on about the houses around him. It was hard to take his eyes off her, dressed in a simple top and shorts, her hair still in the bun from her class. He longed to release it, to run his fingers through her curls but instead was content with holding her hand, watching her experience this lifetime chance.

Had he ever been excited about something as simple as a trip? Hell, he could afford to fly to the Bahamas every month if he chose. Suddenly he found himself excited for her to experience the rest of the trip, to explore the other ports with her at his side. He had already treated her to the ever-popular conch fritters and visited the straw market where she had purchased trinkets before taking her out on the tour of the island, where they were now enjoying rum punch and the beautiful day aboard a catamaran.

"Thank you," she said suddenly, turning toward him. "I wouldn't have enjoyed it near as much without your help. I confess I didn't expect to get off of the ship so I didn't do much research." She then leaned over and kissed him softly on the lips, leaving the taste of rum in its wake.

"You're welcome," he said sincerely, squeezing her hand. Once this was over, would he see life experiences in a different light because of her? Would he just slip back into the shell that was him four days ago, go through life as if nothing else mattered other than the money he would make, the ownership he would eventually garner, the person he would become because of it? What else could he do? He couldn't bring Margaret into his world, his life, without the threat of losing everything he had worked so hard to accomplish. The problem was that he didn't know if he relished in the thought as he had previously.

Chapter 9

Margaret nearly ran to Dominic, knowing that she had one of those goofy grins on her face but she couldn't help it. Yesterday she had experienced things in the Bahamas she would never have experienced without Dominic, followed by a sunset dinner in yet another one of the ship's restaurants. Never had she felt like this, never had she looked forward to seeing someone as much as she did with Dominic.

"Hi," she said breathlessly as she reached him at the meeting spot near the grand staircase. "I've got a surprise for you."

He arched a brow but said nothing, taking her hand as she tugged him into the club. "I know you probably don't like to dance but I thought it would be fun for you to learn, with me."

"Is it the same one we did the first night?" he asked teasingly, pulling her close to him. "I thoroughly enjoyed that one."

"No, I think you have that one down pat," she replied, her cheeks flushed as she remembered how close he had held her. "I am going to teach you the samba."

"Sounds like a disease of some kind," he frowned as she positioned him in front of her. She laughed and swatted at his chest, where he caught her hand and pressed a kiss to her palm, his eyes heated. "Very well, try your best."

Swallowing, she helped him through the initial movements, allowing the music to guide her steps. "Quick, quick, slow," she repeated, showing him how to conquer the sensual dance. "Very good, you are a quick learner." Dominic's feet tangled up with hers and she fell against him, laughing. "Perhaps I spoke too soon."

"I'm wounded," he said, his eyes sparkling devilishly. "I feel you need to make it up to me with a kiss."

Forgetting the lesson, she brought her hand up to his cheek, stroking it softly with her fingers. "You poor thing. I think I can do that." Softly, she pressed her lips to his, feeling the heat flare up between them instantly. He growled against her lips and took control, tasting her until she was moaning in his mouth.

"What you do to me," he said against her lips as they both gulped for air. "Margaret."

"I – I know," she said, clinging to his shirt. She knew all too well.

"Come," he finally said, stepping back and holding out his hand. "I've got plans for an outing today."

***

"Do I have this on right?"

"It's perfect," Dominic replied, adjusting his own goggles. "I can't believe you have never been snorkeling before." He wasn't going to tell her that it had been at least ten years since he had been himself. The water looked clear and inviting and he spotted a number of fish that were waiting to be seen just under the surface of the water. He had rented a snorkeling adventure from the excursion desk and they had left the cruise ship in favor of a small touring boat. The excursion crew had supplied the equipment and they were watching Margaret with amused looks on their faces.

"I've never had the opportunity," she replied, then laughed at his expression. "I know, living in Florida I should have."

"Well, there's no better place than Turks," he responded, grabbing her hand. "Ready?" She nodded and they both jumped into the water from the back of the boat, the warmth of the water like a warm shower on their skin. Dominic pointed down and they swam side by side, Margaret pointing out various colorful sea plants immediately. He was surprised at how relaxed he felt, how the world melted away under the water with Margaret. This morning hadn't started off very well. He had been forced to give an update on his trip, a quick email to George stating that he was close to closing the deal. In truth, the deal was closed, the paperwork sitting in his briefcase on the ship. To keep his secret, he was stretching the truth just a bit.

For Dominic, having to write that email was a reminder of the life that was waiting for him once this ended. There was no Margaret once he disembarked this ship, no dancing, and no more of the exciting experiences that his life had suddenly contained with Margaret. It reminded him of the precious time he had left with her and the deception he was inadvertently forcing upon her. She didn't know of Samantha, and didn't know that there was nothing after the cruise for them. Without marriage to Samantha he could kiss those shares goodbye and any chance to one day own the company. That was why there could be nothing between him and Margaret after this cruise. It was selfish of him to not tell her but watching her enjoy something as simple as snorkeling he couldn't force himself to do anything else but enjoy the present. They broke the surface after a while and she launched into a description of everything she had seen, causing him to grin from her enthusiasm.

"I will never forget this," she smiled as they climbed onboard the small boat and handed off their gear to the crew. He wanted to say the same, looking at her in her bikini, the sun and crystal-blue water framing her. It was a mental picture he wouldn't forget any time soon.

"You're gorgeous," he said, pulling her close despite their wet bodies. Her eyes softened and he kissed her softly. She would never have this with anyone else. He just hoped when they parted that it would not be a bad memory for her. He hoped that when they parted it would not feel like his heart was ripped out of his chest because she was leaving.

***

Margaret made her way to her room, a goofy smile on her face as she relived the snorkeling adventure in her head. After inserting the card into the lock, Margaret pushed open the door and stopped immediately.

"Oh my God."

Margaret held her hand up to her mouth as she looked at the bouquet, the strong smell of roses permeating her cabin. It was a gorgeous arrangement with bright yellow roses on the cusp of opening, a faint line of red on their tips. There was no card but she didn't need one. A soft smile played on her lips as she fingered the velvet petals. This was totally unexpected but that was Dominic. Unpredictable, caring, and unbelievably a dream come true to her. A tear fell from her eye and she dashed it away, willing herself to not cry over what must end. He was from California and she was clear across the country in Florida. He was dedicated to his work and she to hers. Could she move out there with him if he asked?

Were his feelings as strong as hers despite their short time together? She was head over heels in love with the man, that was for sure. Never had she felt like this, never had anyone taken so much time with her to ensure her happiness. Wrapping her hands around her waist, Margaret rapidly blinked, clearing her tears. She could not fall apart now. They still had eight days left and she would savor each one, beginning with tonight.

Chapter 10

"I wish this cruise would go on forever. Think of the places we could see."

Dominic shifted his arm to pull her closer, enjoying the feel of her on his body. They were curled up in one of the lounge chairs on the top deck, looking up at the stars above with Margaret's lithe body draped over his. It was rapidly becoming their favorite pastime after dinner, talking and laughing under the stars as music drifted up from the club below. Sometimes they danced right there on the deck but most of the time they didn't, instead reminiscing on the day's events they had shared together. "I think you would grow tired of it after a while."

"Never," she said, her hand stroking his chest through his shirt absently. "I want to see it all now. When I get back, I am going to start planning for the next one."

He laughed but it was hollow, the thought of her experiencing this without him forming a lump in his throat. He wouldn't be able to do this again, not this way. His next "vacation" would be his honeymoon, then from there he doubted he would have any time to do anything else but work. Stroking her hair with his fingers, he stared up at the sky. "You deserve that, Margaret. Go, do it while you can."

"And you don't?" she asked, picking her head up to look at him. "If anyone, you deserve some fun in your life, Dominic. You should travel, enjoy the fruits of your labor. What's the point of making money if you can't enjoy it some?"

"I wish I could explain it to you, Margaret. Just trust me when I say that this life is not the one I will lead once we are docked."

"That's so sad," she murmured, stroking his jaw with her fingers. "I'm sorry, Dominic." He didn't say anything as he kissed her lightly, doubting that anyone had ever cared about him as she did at this moment. She made him feel, well, special. He was humbled by it.

"Will you take me to your room tonight?"

Startled, he looked at her, thinking he must have made those words up in his head. The telltale blush on her cheeks told him otherwise. "Are you sure?"

"I've never been surer of anything in my entire life," she said softly. "Please."

Chapter 11

Margaret followed Dominic to his suite, her nerves on edge at what she was going to experience. She loved this man and the thought of not sharing her feelings with him broke her heart. He needed her love, he needed to know that she cared about him, his future in the business world as well as his personal life. This man had no doubt worked hard to get where he was at in his profession, but his personal life was seriously lacking. If she wasn't mistaken, he looked just as nervous as she felt.

Dominic inserted his card into one of the doors and threw open the door, moving to let her past.

"No fair," she stated as she took in the large expanse of the room, the size of his balcony. "Your room is so much bigger."

"Feel free to spend as much time as you want here," he said softly, closing the door behind him.

Blushing, she turned toward him. "I confess I haven't done this very often, Dominic."

"Every time should be the first time," he replied, reaching for her. "This is something special between us, Margaret. There be no wrong between us tonight." He kissed her and she melted, clinging to his neck as his lips traveled from hers and down the side of her neck, nipping at her earlobe. "You make me feel as if this is my first time all over again," he breathed into her ear, his hands drifting down her arms, leaving goose bumps in their wake.

"It is my first time with you," she replied, capturing his face in her hands.

He looked at her then, fire in his blue depths. "Then it will be special to both of us."

Margaret nodded as he moved his hands to the tie of her dress, another wrap dress that she had put on with this specifically in mind. She stopped him though, forcing his hands to his sides. "You first. Let me undress you." She wanted him to feel just as special. His face darkened but he left his hands where she had put them.

"I should tell you I'm not very good at following orders in the bedroom."

"I will make it worth your while then." With a smile, she pushed off his coat and undid the tie around his neck, kissing his neck just as he had hers. The hiss that followed told her she had the same effect on him as she untucked his shirt from his dress pants, her fingers nimbly working on the buttons until his entire chest was bared before her. "You're gorgeous," she said reverently, taking in the dips and planes of his honed body. He was hot to the touch as she laid her hands on his chest, her fingers threading through the coarse sparse hair.

Placing a kiss above his heart, she felt him shudder and smiled, never feeling so powerful as a woman as she was feeling at the moment. Her fingers trailed south and she undid his belt buckle, taking her time to pull his pants down until he was standing in his socks and boxers, a sheen of sweat breaking out on his skin. "Are you okay?" she asked, allowing her fingers to trail down his washboard abs.

"You are killing me, Margaret," he said, his jaw clenched tightly. "I will enjoy torturing you just as much when it's my turn."

Shivering, she touched him lightly, feeling him jerk through the thin material. He was big and obviously aroused, growing larger under her light touch.

"Margaret," he warned as she cupped him through his boxers. "This will be over before it starts if you continue to do this."

"I'm sorry," she fumbled, dragging herself up against his body. He grabbed her then, pressing her hard against his nearly naked body.

"Never be sorry with me. Call me selfish but I am ready for my turn with you now." She shrieked then as he picked her up easily, striding to the bed and depositing her on it. She giggled as he nuzzled her neck, his hands deftly undoing the tie around her waist and pulling her dress open. Thank God she had placed all of her cards on the table and wore a pair of her sexiest undergarments just in case. Suddenly, his hands were everywhere on her body, touching her lightly with his fingertips. His mouth was on her breasts, his tongue lavishing her as she writhed under his touch. Suddenly he was touching the very core of her, causing her to cry out as he pleasured her to quick orgasm.

"Dominic." She breathed as he tore off his boxers and made quick work of the rest of her clothing. "Protection."

"I got it," he said, his breath harsh as she heard him ready himself. "This isn't going to be very long, Margaret. I —"

"It's fine," she smiled, touching her hand to his cheek. "We have plenty of time."

He smiled darkly and eased himself in, Margaret lost to the new sensations of Dominic above her, in her. "God you are perfect," he said, kissing her forehead as he began to move.

Margaret clutched his shoulders and pulled him against her, loving the way he felt against her body. "Dominic."

"I'm right here," he said, finding his rhythm. She felt the pressure begin to build within herself, her heart bursting with love for the man above her, loving her.

Moving with him, she held onto him, the slickness of their bodies aiding in the movement.

"Love," she panted, pulling him down to her as she let go. "I love you."

Chapter 12

Dominic looked up at the dark ceiling, feeling the boat rock softly around them. Margaret was curled up next to him, her hand on his chest as she slept in easy slumber. He, on the other hand, was wide wake, his body still humming from their lovemaking. It was lovemaking to her, her declaration shaking him to the very core even hours later. She loved him, Dominic Graham, ruthless businessman and liar. This woman had brought him down to his knees in one earth-shattering moment. He was angry, he was humbled, and he was, hell, he didn't know what he was anymore.

Rubbing a hand over his face, he felt Margaret shift in her sleep, mumbling something close to his name as she threw her leg over his. It was obvious in her sleep she didn't want to let him go and he wasn't so sure that he wanted to let her go either. God, if she found out about his life now she would hate him. Before they slept together it would have been hard to tell her, but after what they just shared, it would be heartbreak. He should have stopped this, pushed her away at the first chance. He should have never pursued her, but heaven help him, he couldn't even regret a single moment.

"I'm so sorry, Margaret," he whispered, leaning over to stroke her hair. He had never been sorry for anything in his life, not the people he had stepped on to climb the ladder, not the way he had shunned his family or his friends. He hadn't been sorry for the way he had used Samantha to get George's attention but this, this he was sorry for. Margaret was innocent, special, and he would crush her. For her sake he would have to push her away eventually, break it off before the cruise ended. He couldn't offer her a relationship; he couldn't give her what she deserved. It would eat him alive long after he left her.

Chapter 13

Margaret opened her eyes to the bright sunshine, stretching out the kinks in her body as her surroundings came into focus. Oh Lord. This was not her room and as the past evening's events slipped into her mind, she found herself blushing. She remembered the tender lovemaking and the way Dominic had teased her with demanding kisses. The man amazed her. Sitting up, she found his side empty and the clock informing her she had two hours before her class, which would give her plenty of time to shower and change. Then she could spend the day with the man she loved, the man that had captured her heart.

With a sigh, Margaret fell back onto the pillows, reliving the night before in her mind. She had thrown caution to the wind, telling him that she loved him, and did not regret it one bit. Love was a precious thing and even if he didn't return the sentiment, then at least she had known true love once in her lifetime. She wasn't expecting a future with Dominic and there was a good chance that at the end of this cruise she would be the one leaving with a broken heart. She had fallen too hard and fast without pause to think how this relationship was going to work out beyond this cruise. Besides, she didn't know whether he was looking only to spend time with someone to ease the boredom or truly looking for a relationship outside of this trip. It was something she would have to learn to live with unfortunately but the memories she would have!

Perhaps she was being too cynical, Margaret thought as she climbed out of the bed in search of her clothing. Maybe, just maybe she had reached Dominic's heart as well and he wanted a relationship with her.

"Margaret, you are crazy," she said to herself, pushing back the hair off her forehead. She had known Dominic all of a week if that and now she had gone and fallen in love with him. It was something she felt for him, the way he brought out the best in her.

Laughing, Margaret pushed herself off the bed, her face burning now as she realized how her clothes were strewn about the room. She had been very straightforward last night, which was out of character for her, but had enjoyed it, really enjoyed it. The door opened and she squeaked, pulling on her wrap as fast as she could.

"Good morning."

Relieved that it was Dominic and not the attendant, Margaret gave him a bright smile as she drank in the sight of him. He was clad only in a pair of running shorts and sneakers, his bare chest glistening with sweat. There was a smirk on his handsome face and Margaret felt her cheeks pinken under his gaze. Whatever brave, empowered woman she had been last night was very hard to replicate when the sun was up. "Good morning," she finally said, finding her voice. "I was just about to take a shower. In my own room." The smile was predatory as Dominic advanced on her, her heart hammering with each step he took. She had very little time to react as he grabbed her, his mouth crushing hers hungrily. He tasted of sweat and mint, his mouth roaming over hers until her knees were weak with need.

"Why waste water when you could take a shower with me?" Dominic breathed into her ear, his lips placing small kisses along the delicate shell. "I can assure you it will be a hell of a lot more fun if you do."

"But I don't have any toiletries," Margaret stammered though her hands were already trailing over his bare shoulders, still warm from the morning sun. She would never grow tired of touching his body.

"I can share my toiletries every once in a while," Dominic said, nipping her shoulder as he tugged on at the ties of her dress. "Join me, Margaret."

"Well if you insist," she grinned, kissing the underside of his jaw, feeling the roughness of the stubble on her tender lips. Dominic's eyes darkened as he finally finagled her dress off of her body, his hands sliding over her bare skin in the lightest caress. "How long do we have?"

"Two hours before my class," she gasped as he leaned down to kiss her.

"A challenge, I like it," he grinned wickedly, scooping her up into his arms before striding to the bathroom, much to Margaret's cry of delight. "A two-hour shower, hmm? I've never thought of that before." Oh boy, she thought as she wrapped her arm around his neck. This was going to be an enjoyable two hours.

Chapter 14

After their wickedly entertaining two-hour shower that ended up being spent more in the bed then the actual bathroom, Dominic had escorted Margaret to her class. Now he watched as she danced with her current partner, educating her pupils on the fine points of a proper samba. If he had to stay in the same spot for the rest of his life, he didn't think he would ever grow tired of watching her dance. With every movement, every smile he could see that she really enjoyed this trade, that this was what she was born to do. In this element, she nearly glowed.

Taking a slow breath, Dominic watched as she rolled her hips, his body tightening in response. God she was gorgeous, her hair piled on top of her head in some haphazard bun, the sundress twirling about her body as she moved to the music. It had been Margaret that he had thought about on his run this morning, the taste of her, the smell of her engrained in his pores. Any guilt he had felt from the night together had vanished when he had seen her in his room, that beautiful smile on her face. All thoughts of ending this, minimizing her hurt had disappeared with one look.

Margaret was something special and God help him, Dominic wanted to hang onto her for as long as he could. He wanted to show her a side of him that he didn't even know had existed before her, to closet themselves from the harsh reality that would be their lives once this trip was finished. There was nothing, not words or money or gifts, that would change how she felt about him once the truth was out about his engagement and he was certain it would reach her eventually. She would have questions, she would be hurt, and he didn't know what to do about it. A better man would walk away now but he couldn't, not now.

"Hello, gorgeous, thinking of what you are going to dazzle me with today?"

His mouth curving into a smile, Dominic watched as Margaret moved toward him, her toned body gliding across the floor like a sleek panther. His hands itched to touch every dip and crevice, remembering how their morning had gotten started. "You dazzle me with just your presence alone," he said easily.

"You need to work on your cheesy lines," she laughed, rising on her toes to plant a kiss on his lips. "But I appreciate it anyway."

He laughed then, grabbing her by the waist to satisfy the sheer need to touch her in some way, dipping her low to the floor. "I do not care what we do today but I want to go dancing tonight, with you."

"I'm sure we can arrange something," she smiled, grabbing his hand and leading him out of the club.

"I've got a proposition for today but I'm not sure if you would like to partake."

"As long as it has nothing to do with waxing I'm game," Dominic grinned as she pulled him down the passageway and into the grand atrium.

"Good," she said as they climbed the stairs to the next level. Once he saw the spa entrance, he couldn't help but laugh, tugging on her arm in an effort to get her to stop. "Couples massage with me doing the massage, right?" He was dying to get his hands on her body once more, his lust for her seeming to be never sated.

"I doubt much massaging would be going on for too long," she replied, looking at him with a wicked grin. "I thought we both could use a relaxing day so I booked us some spa treatments. Massages, facials, whatever you like."

Dominic pulled her against him, kissing her softly. It was a simple thought, but for Dominic it spoke volumes. He couldn't remember the last time someone had thought of his comfort that he wasn't paying to do so. He was used to being wined and dined but not for the pleasure of his company. "Thank you." Later he would come back and ensure that the bill was charged to his room. He had seen the prices. The spa treatments, while top of the line, were an extra on the cruise that would be expensive for someone on Margaret's budget.

"Don't thank me until afterward," she smiled, stepping out of his embrace, her eyes sparkling. "Watch out for the tweezers and hot wax."

"Minx," he laughed, allowing her to pull him through the doors.

Chapter 15

Hours later Margaret stood in the doorway of the club, a giddy smile on her face as she looked for a familiar form. She had been plucked, painted, and massaged to the point of sheer oblivion but when she had finished, Dominic had been nowhere to be found. He had left a note, telling her to enjoy herself and to meet him at this club, a pulsating Latino-themed club that Margaret had yet to try out. She just hoped that he had enjoyed himself. Dominic reminded her of a man who rarely did any relaxation for himself and she wanted to give him something for what he had done for her in providing the experiences on this cruise so far. A nice, long nap had ensued after she had left the spa and now Margaret, refreshed and energized, was ready for a fun night with the love of her life. Everyone back home would think she was crazy for what she was feeling in the short amount of time that she had known Dominic. After all, their first encounter hadn't gone very well. It seemed like a lifetime ago now.

"Mmm, you look beautiful."

Margaret smiled as Dominic's arms came around her, his lips nuzzling her bare neck as he pulled her against him possessively. She had taken extra care in dressing tonight, pulling out her sexiest dress with him in mind. The short coral sheath showed off her toned legs and great tan and Margaret had chosen to leave her hair down, knowing that he preferred it that way. Turning in his arms, she encircled her arms around his neck, playing with the hair at the nape.

"Where did you run off to earlier? I wanted to see what color they painted your nails."

"I had something I had to do," he said, kissing her on the lips. "I came by your room but you didn't answer."

"I fell asleep," she said sheepishly. "So you enjoyed my surprise?"

Dominic's eyes were warm as he fingered her curls, wrapping one around his finger. "I did. Thank you. It was exactly what I needed." Glad that he had liked it, Margaret stepped back, admiring his form encased in a dress shirt the color of his eyes and dark pants. He looked, well, good enough to eat. Tamping down her desire, Margaret tucked her arm in his instead, enjoying the closeness of their skin. "So shall we butt in on this dance?"

"I've got a better idea," he said, pulling her back toward the entrance.

"But I thought you wanted to dance?" she asked, puzzled. Wasn't that why they were here?

"Oh I do," he said, his voice warm and low, sending shivers over her bare skin. "But not here. Trust me, Margaret."

On edge, Margaret allowed him to lead her away from the club and toward the front of the ship. They passed the pool and hot tubs, where a few people still lounged, and through a door she hadn't seen before. A narrow hallway stood before them and Dominic started down the hallway, his steps sure and deliberate as he led her through another door and out into the night once more.

"Oh my God," she breathed as she realized they were at the front of the ship, under a small alcove with nothing but the vast ocean before them.

"You surprised me so it was my turn to do the same," he said softly as she took in the picnic-like setting before her. "I wanted a table but was informed that it was not an option, so I compromised."

"This is wow," she stated as he led her over to the blanket situated on the deck floor near the wall with a soft outside light right above their heads. The light was enough not to be fumbling in the darkness, but cozy enough to provide them some privacy.

"Shh, listen," he said wrapping his arm around her waist. Over the sound of the boat slicing through the water she could hear the faint sound of a sweet melody, one that warranted the slowest of dances.

"How did you…?" she began as he pulled her close against him.

"Lots of persuasion," he grinned, his fingers drifting down the open back of her dress. "And a Bluetooth speaker borrowed from one of the crew members. I told you I wanted to dance. I just didn't tell you where."

Shaking her head she started to move with him, slowly to enjoy the feel of their bodies against each other. He gathered her hand and held it close to his heart as Margaret rested her cheek against his chest, overwhelmed by the emotions she was feeling at this moment. This was unexpected and had caught her unaware, much like she had this morning to him. Under her cheek she could feel his faint heartbeat, his warmth that radiated from his body. All of the worry about what was going to happen once they left this cruise melted away in this singular moment, just the two of them under the stars. It was perfect.

"Shh, don't cry. This was supposed to be a good moment," Dominic said softly.

"I-I'm not crying," Margaret sniffed, realizing in fact that a tear had escaped her eye. "Okay, maybe I am."

Bringing his hand up to her neck, Dominic forced her to look at him, kissing their joined hands as he looked into her eyes. "This was for you, Margaret. I wanted you to have a perfect moment to this perfect cruise."

Margaret looked at the simple, but very sweet gesture of a picnic, then up at the stars above, dozens upon dozens in the clear night sky. The whole gesture was perfect. She didn't need fancy restaurants or exotic locales, all she needed to feel was that he cared for her and this setting was the perfect example. "How did you get so wonderful?" she asked, her tears now safely locked away. She didn't want to ruin this moment between them.

"I'm not always like this," he said, a shadow crossing his face. "But you have brought something out in me and I want to say thank you."

"It's perfect," she smiled, squeezing his hand. Dominic smiled then and released her, pulling her down on the blanket.

"Come on. Let's eat before they kick us out. I am good at persuasion but only for an hour or two." Margaret laughed then as she knelt on the blanket, watching as he brought out various wrapped containers and a plastic carafe of red wine. "They wouldn't let me have glass out here either," he said sheepishly, handing her a plastic cup instead. "I think they were scared I was going to do something crazy like break the glass on the bow or something."

"It's fine," she laughed as he poured the wine into her cup. Settling back, Margaret took the wrapped container and looked up at the clear night sky above, her heart bursting with love for the man next to her. Long after this cruise was over, she would have this memory, regardless of what happened between them. Scooting over, Margaret laid her head on Dominic's shoulder. He in turn placed his hand on her thigh, drawing small patterns on her bare skin. Margaret sighed happily as she felt the warmth of his skin on hers. "Can I ask you a question?"

"Fire away," he replied.

"Who are you really, Dominic? I feel like you are holding back on me."

"There isn't much I haven't told you," he said slowly. "Businessman from Cali, all work and very little play. I thought we had already established that my passion was work just as yours is dancing."

"What about your family, your friends?" Margaret pushed, wanting to know something, anything.

"Only child, parents both retired and living on a golf course in Cali as well," Dominic laughed. "Trust me, Margaret, my life is rather boring. I've amassed a great deal of money, enough to last for a number of years but it's the need to succeed that keeps me coming back for more."

Margaret was silent for a moment, thinking about what he had said. Was she in that same bucket? Was it his need to "succeed" in getting her in his bed that had kept him around? Was all of this some grand show in an effort to keep her in his bed at night? Somehow she didn't think so. She had to find out what his thoughts were for the future, if there was any future for them. She desperately wanted one. "This thing between us, do you see it moving past this cruise?"

***

Dominic stiffened at Margaret's innocent question, warning lights going off in his head. His body screamed for him to answer yes, to tell her he would see her outside of this vacation. He wanted to continue whatever it was they were experiencing, to see her love for him grow. Life would be a constant surprise with Margaret, every day a new adventure full of feelings he hadn't experienced with anyone else. He could almost see how she would react to some of the places he could take her to, how she would make him enjoy it just as much as she did and see life in a new light. He could see her riding along the coast in his convertible, her hair blowing in the breeze. He could give her so much, yet Dominic didn't see Margaret overlooking the fact that he was already in a relationship that was about to progress to marriage. "We live on opposite ends of the country," he said slowly, trying to have her see the barriers they were faced with.

"Yes, I know," she said softly, fiddling with her cup. "I was thinking about that and if, I mean if you think…"

"What?" Dominic interrupted, his body taut with the entire conversation. What was she thinking? What was her take on how to keep this going?

"I could move out west," she replied, so quietly that he almost couldn't hear her over the ocean. "I would be closer at least and there's nothing in Florida really tying me down. I don't know if you think that would be something that you would want me to do."

The very thought humbled him. She was willing to pull up her stakes and move out west to continue this relationship. "What about your dancing? Your job?" he asked, his own voice sounding foreign to his ears. He would have her out there in an instant if he could. The thought of having Margaret in his bed, in his world appealed to him in a way that he had never felt before. It just couldn't happen. His life would be ruined if he didn't marry Samantha. George would not look very kindly upon his number one dumping his only daughter and still expect to be the owner of the corporation one day. That was still his goal, wasn't it?

"Those things can be easily done in California," Margaret was saying, her fingers drifting over the back of his hand in a lazy pattern. "I'm sorry, this is stupid. Forget I ever said anything."

Dominic shifted his weight and looked at her, seeing the hurt and embarrassment in her eyes. He knew it wasn't the answer she was hoping for and he was at a loss to handle what she was feeling at the moment. "It's not that," he started, reaching up to stroke her cheek. "You have a life in Florida. By what you have told me, you have clients that adore you, how could they not?"

"If you don't want me out there, just say so, Dominic. Quit beating around the bush."

"It's not easy out there," he said honestly, thinking of the struggles he had to overcome to get where he was now. Margaret would survive, he was sure of it but she wouldn't be happy and he couldn't protect her from the storm of what his life really did entail once they stepped off this boat. One word that he was already taken would send this relationship to the dump and then she would be stuck out there. Could he watch her with another man? Could he watch her succeed in her life without him? In another time he would move her in, give her everything she could possibly want and ride this thing out for as long as it would go. He wasn't free to do that and never would be. He could give her false hope for the moment, he supposed, the thought of lying to Margaret souring his stomach. In the end, he took the only way out that he knew. "We will see each other after this trip, Margaret. We will work this out."

Chapter 16

"Grab your sneakers. We leave in ten minutes."

Margaret groaned and buried her head under the covers, hoping that Dominic would just climb back in the bed and let her sleep in for once. Her normal morning dance class would be cancelled today due to the deck party this evening, where she and another crew member from the entertainment team would entertain the crowd with their dancing. "Go away. It's my day to sleep in."

"Not today," Dominic replied, pulling the covers back, the cold air hitting her naked body. "Come on, sleepyhead. This is our last stop, remember? The excursion leaves in ten minutes and you can either come dressed or like this."

Margaret lifted her head to face him, sticking her tongue out at his playful gaze. "You wouldn't dare take me out there without any clothes on."

Dominic lifted a brow as he reached for her, sending her squealing to the other end of the bed. "Don't tempt me, Margaret. You have no idea what I might do."

Laughing, she made herself get out of the bed, stretching in front of him.

"Ten minutes, Margaret."

"Fine, fine." Gathering the bag she had packed last night, Margaret went into Dominic's bathroom and shut the door. After their impromptu picnic, the conversation had drifted to more mundane topics, but Dominic's reaction to her suggestion, his vague answer still stayed with her. It shouldn't hurt as much as it did, after all they weren't truly in a relationship, but she had laid it all on the line for just a simple yes and instead Dominic had walked around the question and his answer. She had smiled, laughed, and made passionate love, all the while the thought of their conversation hanging over her head and like a shadow on her heart.

"Get a grip, Margaret," she said to her reflection in the mirror, the woman who looked in love with the man on the other side of the door. This was a fling, a vacation fling that she would smile and walk away from in the end, regardless of how she felt about him. Dominic must think she was crazy for asking! Sighing, she pulled out the outfit he said she needed for today, her bikini and a tank/shorts combo that would be comfortable. All of this worrying about what the future held was going to ruin the precious time that she could be showing him just how much he was going to miss her once they walked down that ramp in Florida.

Dressing quickly, Margaret performed her basic toilette before opening the door, finding Dominic standing just on the other side, his arms crossed over his chest. "What? I got ready in five minutes?"

"You know we can't do anything in five minutes," he grinned, handing her sneakers over. "I lied anyway. You still have ten minutes."

"You dolt," she laughed, slipping on her sneakers. "Come on then. At least we will be early instead of late."

With a laugh of his own, Dominic grabbed her hand and their backpacks before heading out of the room. "So what is this excursion anyway?" she asked as they moved through the ship to the port side, where the gangplank was set up to allow access to the dock.

"Let's see," he started as they exited the ship and out into the brilliant sunshine. "There's a jungle, a waterfall, and a beach."

"Well, two out of three isn't bad," she said, tucking her arm in his. "No, I'm excited, really excited. I mean who is to say I will ever get to do these things again?

"I hope you still feel the same after the day is over," Dominic replied, transferring his arm to her waist, pulling her close as they reached the jeep that would take them to their destination. This would be hard to forget. After today, five days remained of this trip;

four nights to spend with Dominic in his bed before they would have to say goodbye. She could do this, could love this man with every fiber of her being even if their relationship were meant to end once they docked back in Florida.

Chapter 17

"This is unbelievable. Have you ever seen anything so beautiful?"

Dominic watched as Margaret took multiple pictures of the waterfall before them, the setting something out of a movie. It was beautiful, but his attention was on the woman before him more than the waterfall. It had taken them a little over an hour to hike to it, the sights and sounds of the jungle all around them. Margaret had talked nearly the entire time as their guide showed them the way, never once complaining about the heat or the walk. In fact, she looked like she had enjoyed every solitary moment of this excursion. "Too bad we can't do some skinny dipping underneath that waterfall." Dominic couldn't believe that the tour guide had actually addressed the subject of skinny dipping in his spiel earlier. Apparently he hadn't been the first man to think along those lines.

"You would think that, wouldn't you," she laughed, climbing off the rock and into his waiting arms. "Hi."

"Hi yourself," Dominic said, kissing her on her nose. "I have seen something beautiful like this before. I believe she was doing the waltz."

"Always a charmer," Margaret smiled, running her hand through his hair as he set her gently on the ground, not releasing her just yet.

Margaret's smile dimmed a little as she searched his face, her hand drifting to his cheek before he kissed her, his mind thinking of all the things he was going to miss about her. She had become something special to him. "This has been the most entertaining, fulfilling vacation I have ever had," he said softly, nibbling at the corner of her mouth. "And it's all because of you, Margaret."

"I think you would have enjoyed it without me," she said softly, all of her emotions reflecting in her depths.

"No," he replied. "Not even close."

"I'm falling for you so bad," Margaret said in a rush, looking away. "I can't help it, Lord knows I've tried to stop it but it's happening."

Dominic's breath stalled in his chest as he heard her admission, remembering the way he had felt when she had told him this the first night they had slept together. It made him feel lower than low at what was going to happen in the end. She would hate him for breaking her heart. At least he would be on the other side of the country when it happened. He wouldn't have to see tears in her eyes as she realized that he had been keeping a terrible secret from her, the real reason he hadn't been able to commit to her or any future she might have wanted. "You humble me, Margaret," he replied, kissing her. "Any man would be lucky to have you by his side."

"Any man or you?" she asked quietly.

"Margaret, I can't answer to you right now. It's difficult."

"No, it's fine," she smiled, though the smile didn't quite reach her eyes. "I shouldn't have tricked you into answering."

Dominic closed his eyes against the onslaught of pain in his chest, her trusting voice nearly tearing him apart. It wasn't going to work out like she hoped. He couldn't dwell on that. As much as he would love to continue this relationship outside of this cruise, there were too many obstacles. Right now he didn't want to waste their precious time together figuring out the what-ifs when they docked back in Florida. He wanted to enjoy Margaret, the wonderful, vivacious woman who had turned his life on its end and was allowing him to live for the first time. "Come on, let's go to the beach," he said instead, keeping his voice level. She would never know the turmoil inside of him. She would never know how hard leaving her was going to be. She had changed his life.

***

Thirty minutes later Margaret walked up to the small gift shop on the beach, armed with a small amount of cash for snacks and waters. Though the day was perfect weather, she wasn't enjoying it as much as she would have liked. Dominic was fighting something internally, his answers to her questions only leading to more questions.

Grabbing a couple of waters and some granola bars, Margaret paused at the checkout, seeing the man of her thoughts on the cover of a business magazine. "The future of Hamilton International," it read under the picture. He was seated in a leather office chair, his expression pensive as he looked out of a large paned-glass window. This was the man she didn't know. Snatching it up, she put it with the other things, biting her lip as she paid for their snacks and the magazine. The Dominic she knew was laughing most of the time now, his eyes lighting up when they spied her. This man on the cover looked cold and distant. Perhaps she could glean some information later from the article. She wanted to know both sides of Dominic: the fun-loving man she had been privy to as well as the serious businessman that kept his private life hidden.

With a sigh, Margaret tucked the magazine under her arm as she headed back to the chairs, where Dominic and that fantastic body of his lay stretched out in the tropical sun. He was so hot it hurt her to even look at him sometimes. Taking the water bottle, Margaret rolled it gently on his skin, laughing when he abruptly sat up with a yelp.

"You minx," he laughed, reaching for her. "That was very cold."

"You looked hot," she said as she tumbled on top of him, the delicious friction of bare skin causing her heart to pound in her ears. He grabbed her around the waist and squeezed, holding her against him as she swatted at his shoulder. It had never been like this with anyone else, this sensation that she hoped would never grow old. "Let me up, people are starting to stare."

"One kiss and I will release you," he said with a naughty grin. The moment their lips met something inside Margaret shifted and she moaned, wrapping her arms around his neck as he nibbled on the sides of her mouth, teasing her relentlessly. "Too bad everyone is looking," he whispered as his lips moved up to the shell of her ear. "I could take you right here in the sand, Margaret."

"I think we would be arrested then," she gasped as his lips moved back down to the side of her jaw, where he nipped a path to her mouth.

"Would you care?"

"Probably not," she grinned, meeting his eyes. She saw warmth, affection, desire; all of the things any girl wants to see in the man that she loved. "Can't we just stay here forever?" Dominic looked around them, his arms tightening around her as she leaned against his shoulder, unspoken words hanging between them.

Chapter 18

Dominic watched as Margaret tipped her head back in contentment, her hand squeezing his lightly. They were sitting on his balcony, the stars their only companions. It was late but he wasn't tired, wanting to enjoy every solitary moment with Margaret. They had enjoyed a nice late dinner in one of the restaurants after her live performance on the deck. She had danced in perfect rhythm with her partner and Dominic hadn't been able to take his eyes off her. He enjoyed watching her dance, the passion for dancing showing in every step. She had then left him to change her clothes and he had been wowed by her simple black strapless dress and come-hither heels that already had him hot and bothered. Her conversation during dinner had made him laugh more times than he cared to admit, telling him of her antics in her younger days. She had lived a happy life, even without a ton of money to show for it.

Dominic had found himself questioning his choices, like the choice to marry Samantha. In truth she was his type, understood his ambitions and drive to success. He cared for her, liked her, but he had never felt with her anything similar to what he felt Margaret. Margaret made him forget the man he was and showed him the man he could be. Samantha showed him what he had always strived to achieve and what his future would hold. Without Samantha, he had no future with Hamilton, all of the years he had busted his ass would be gone. But without Margaret, he would return to that empty shell of a life. There would be no laughter, no true enjoyment in life. Margaret was his light in the dark world. Looking at her, he couldn't help but feel as if she was what made him complete, his other half. Dammit, he loved her. The realization struck him hard. He loved her. These feelings couldn't be anything else but love.

"Come here," he said to her, tugging on her arm. She gave him that dazzling smile that punched him in the gut as she slid her arms around his neck, fitting perfectly in his lap.

"What? Is there something you want?"

"I want you," he said roughly as his hands inched up her skirt.

"We can't do it out here on this balcony," she protested with very little fight, sighing as his fingers found what they were looking for.

"Think of it as a memory," he whispered in her ear, his heart wanting to tell her how he felt. He couldn't get the words out, his throat clogged with emotion. He didn't deserve her. Finding her mouth, Dominic forced all of the jumbled thoughts aside. He would show her in his actions how much he loved her.

Chapter 19

Margaret fell back on her bed with a sigh, her body stretched from her morning dance class. Today had been the jive, which tended to be more taxing than some of her other dances. Thankfully, her class had enjoyed the challenge with enthusiasm and determination and by the end, they all walked away happy. It was that satisfaction that kept her teaching. Rolling onto her side, Margaret knew she had to get up. Dominic had left her to go work out in the gym after her dance class and Margaret had come to her room to take a small nap. Rested, she now was looking forward to another day with Dominic.

Spying the magazine she had bought on a whim, Margaret picked it up, grinning as she looked at Dominic's handsome profile on the cover. He reminded her of the prickly man she had encountered in the diner, not the man who had spent the evening laughing and talking about her childhood while enjoying dinner.

Flipping it open, Margaret thumbed through until she found the article, excitement and nervousness building within. This was going to give her a glimpse into his other world and she wasn't sure how she felt about it. The article began, "When one thinks of the future, Dominic Graham's name has to be thrown into the ring. As the current CEO of Hamilton International, Dominic Graham has proven a thousand times over that he is a force to be reckoned with."

"Well, at least he wasn't lying about the CEO part," Margaret smiled.

The article continued, "While Mr. Graham is the youngest and brightest CEO to touch Hamilton International since its inception, one might think he is on the fast track to owner, replacing the great George Hamilton himself. While Mr. Graham has proven himself to be a shrewd businessman, it can't hurt that he has won the hand of the owner's daughter with the lavish wedding to take place next month."

Margaret's smile faded to confusion as she reread the phrase, an unsettling feeling in her gut. Surely not. Dominic would have told her if he was engaged. She had given him many times to talk about his other life, even before they had slept together. Turning the page, Margaret dropped the magazine on the bed, seeing the proof right before her eyes. It was a picture of Dominic, dressed to the nines as he escorted a tall blonde into a charity function. In any other picture she would have thought them just acquaintances, but the joining of hands and the massive diamond twinkling in the camera shot told her everything she needed to know.

Feeling nauseated, Margaret put her head in her hands, the tears threatening to spill over. He had lied to her. No, he hadn't lied, he had deliberately withheld the fact that he was to be married to another woman! She had slept with and fallen in love with a man who was already taken. What was she going to do? What was she going to say when she saw him?

"I can't believe this," Margaret moaned, wiping the tears that were now coursing down her cheeks. This was the last thing she had expected. She was angry, devastated, and upset. Dominic had not once let on that this was his other life! Was he in love with this woman? Had he been secretly laughing behind Margaret's back the entire time? She had to confront him obviously but the thought made her sick to her stomach. She had kissed this man, made love to this man and all the while he belonged to someone else. There was no happily ever after for them now. No wonder he could never tell her what was going to happen after this cruise. No wonder he had shot her down when she had offered to pick up and move out west to be closer to him. She had always felt like he had withheld part of his life and now she understood why. She hadn't expected it to be this, she hadn't expected it to hurt so unbelievably much.

***

Dominic strolled down the hall to Margaret's room, hoping that she hadn't forgotten they were supposed to meet for lunch. He had waited in his room for over an hour for her to arrive, surprised when her smiling face didn't cross the threshold. His thoughts had ranged from her falling asleep to something was terribly wrong and now his curiosity was getting the better of him.

Knocking softly at her door, he put on a smile as he heard her moving around inside. When she did open the door, he knew instantly something was wrong. Her normally sparkling eyes were red, her face puffy and tear-stained. "What is it? What's wrong?" he asked, his gut a pit of worry. Was she sick, had someone done something to upset her? Whatever it was, he would fix it.

"I don't want to see you right now."

That was not what he had anticipated coming out of her mouth. "Whatever it is, babe, we will fix it," he said, reaching for her. When she shrank from his touch, Dominic felt the first spark of annoyance. Margaret never had rejected his touch before. "Margaret, you have to tell me what's wrong."

"Here," she said angrily, forcing a magazine at him. "This should give you all the information you need." Before he could react, she pushed at his chest, causing him to stumble back before she shut the door, the sound of the lock sliding into place. Dumbfounded, Dominic looked down at the magazine, realizing that he was staring at himself on the cover, a picture from a board meeting no doubt. Was she mad that he was on the cover? Flipping through the pages, it didn't take him long to realize what she was really upset about

"Margaret, we need to talk," he said, knocking on the door, barely constraining the need to break the door down. "I – I need to explain this."

"There's nothing to explain," she said, her voice muffled from the solid door between them. "Unless the article is lying."

"I – dammit, Margaret, open the door," Dominic demanded, resting his forehead on the cool wood. This was not how he had wanted her to find out. He didn't know what to say, what to do to ease the hurt she was feeling. He was hurting too, knowing that she had found out this way, a silly article that had exposed the truth about his life. "Please, let me explain. I know you are upset." The door flew open and Dominic nearly fell inside, finding a teary-eyed Margaret pointing at his chest with one trembling finger.

"Upset? I'm not upset. I'm devastated, Dominic! You're – you're engaged for God's sake! You let me believe, you slept with me and all the while you were taken! How could you do that to me! How could you do that to your poor fiancée!"

"It's not what you think," Dominic tried as she backed him up against the hallway wall. "I don't feel this way about her."

"So you are telling me you are over with her?" she asked, some of the anger fading into confusion. "Were you going to end it?"

"I – I can't do that," Dominic answered truthfully. "My entire future is wrapped up in my personal life. You should know, you read the article."

"Oh my God, are you serious?" she exploded, tears running down her cheeks. Dominic's heart broke as he saw her anguish, unable to know how to fix it, how to make it better. In his CEO position, his job was to ensure everything ran smoothly, that the deal closed, but Margaret wasn't a deal. Margaret was real life.

"I didn't get past the fact you are engaged! I can't believe this! You could have stopped this before we slept together, Dominic, but instead you strung me along, like some, some lovesick pup!"

"Margaret, please let me explain," Dominic tried again, gently grabbing her shoulders. He had to calm her down, he had to get her to listen before she did anything rash. The slap came out of nowhere and he reeled back, his hands sliding from her shoulders.

"Don't you dare touch me," she said raggedly, holding her hand. Dominic felt the sting of the slap on his cheek, but it paled in comparison to the pain he saw written all over Margaret's face, pain that he had caused. "Leave me alone."

"Margaret, please," he started as she marched into the room and shut the door, the lock sounding harsh in his ears. "We will talk about this," he said to the closed door, knowing that she was on the other side. He just needed to let her calm down to where they could talk about this in a rational manner. He would explain his side of things, attempt to tell her how he felt about Samantha, about how his future hinged on their marriage. He would tell her how he felt about her as well. "Dammit," he swore, walking away from her door. This was what he had been afraid of. This was losing her without controlling the situation. This was worse than losing any business deal in his career.

Chapter 20

Margaret threw her clothes into her suitcase, ignoring the knock on her door once again. She knew who it was, who it had been for the last two days and she had no interest in seeing him face-to-face. She had successfully dodged him at her last two classes, refusing to acknowledge his presence and always walking with her class attendees after their session in an effort to avoid any awkward confrontation. The flowers he had sent went directly into the trash, the notes torn up and thrown out of the balcony door into the ocean. Her meals had consisted of room service and she couldn't wait another moment to get off of this boat and back to her normal life, well away from the man who had broken her heart in two.

Wiping a stray tear from her eye, Margaret sat down on her bed, wishing that tomorrow would hurry up and come. Tomorrow she would be back on dry land, back with those who would never do these things to her. She would be back in the place where she could start the healing process, the process where she would wipe Dominic Graham out of her memory and out of her heart once and for all. Somehow it sounded a lot easier than she expected it to actually be.

The knocking ceased and Margaret let out a breath, feeling tired. Her first night back in her lonely bed two nights ago had dissolved into a night of crying instead of sleeping. She hadn't realized how much she had gotten used to Dominic sleeping next to her, how she would wake up and see his face each morning. Now all there was an empty pillow and a lifetime of regret. Why hadn't he just told her in the beginning? She might have still hung out with him as friends but at least she would have known he was taken by someone already. There was no bone in her body that made her feel good about what they had shared now knowing he had a fiancée waiting for his return. Margaret would forever be labeled as the other woman, even if she and Dominic were the only ones who knew it. It wasn't a good title to hold. With a sigh, Margaret turned back to her packing. The perfect time in her life had turned sour in an instant. All she could do now was pray for morning to come quickly.

Chapter 21

Dominic pushed on his sunglasses and walked down the ramp to the pavement, his eyes forever scanning the crowds of people before him as he finally stepped onto the shore of Florida. He had tried to talk to Margaret, tried to get her to listen to him to no avail. She hadn't returned his notes, she hadn't answered the door and he highly suspected that all of the flowers ended up in the trash. Now was the day to leave and get on with his life and he couldn't get past the fact that he wouldn't be seeing her again. He wouldn't kiss those lips he knew so well, he wouldn't hold her close at night, and he wouldn't be enjoying any new adventures with her by his side. His heart was heavy with regret, his stomach feeling as if someone had punched him hard. He was going to have leave Florida with this hanging over his head, no resolution in sight. He had tried to hold out for as long as he could on the ship's floor for disembarkment this morning, but even after the majority of the passengers had left, he still hadn't seen her. His only other option was to leave himself.

"Mr. Graham. Your car is waiting over here to take you to the airport, sir."

Dominic nodded at the man to his right who was pushing the cart containing Dominic's luggage. This was it. He had no other choice but to climb in the car and go home, back to the life that was before this cruise.

With a frustrated sigh, Dominic looked back at the boat, his heart hammering in his chest as he watched Margaret exit the ramp. He looked back at the car then at her, his feet wanting to move her way. She looked radiant, her long dark hair in that simple ponytail he loved so much. Her white shorts and tank top showed off her great tan and she was smiling at the crew member beside her as he carried her bags. He wanted to go to her, scoop her up and run back onto the ship where they would have a chance to talk. He wanted to tell her everything, how he was confused about his feelings about Samantha, how he wanted his job but wanted her as well. He wanted to finally be able to tell her that he loved her and see the love for him returned tenfold. He had screwed up whatever relationship they had royally and he just wanted a chance to redeem himself in her eyes.

She looked his way suddenly and he ceased to breathe, hoping that she would acknowledge him in some way to let him know she still cared. Instead, she turned her head sharply, steering away from him and out of sight, giving him the answer he was dreading. She was over him, over whatever special thing they had. She wasn't going to take his engagement lightly and Dominic couldn't blame her. He hadn't told her the truth about his relationship, he hadn't given her any inkling that he might be already attached. Instead he had seen something he had wanted and had taken it, without thinking of the consequences that would eventually come to light. And now he was suffering for it, right along with Margaret. Swearing, Dominic climbed into the cool interior of the car and rested his head against the seat. He had no other choice. He would go back home and eventually forget about the woman who had changed his life.

Chapter 22

Three days later

"Dom, can we talk?" Dominic rubbed his tired eyes with his hand as he saw Samantha in the doorway, a tentative smile on her lovely face. For three days since he had been back in California, he had tried to get back into the swing of things, back to this life he had known before Margaret, but his heart was not in it. He had tried to conjure up the feelings he had thought he had with Samantha, but those seemed suspiciously absent now. She was still Samantha, but he wasn't the same Dominic and it was tearing him up inside. Feelings he hadn't known before were making him question his entire life, the hurt of losing Margaret still weighing heavily on his mind and in his heart. He had thought coming back to his normal, everyday life would lessen the hurt but nothing, not even the successful acquisition of the company in Florida, had given him the high he had once known.

"Sure, come on in." It was late and he was surprised to see her still at the office, her suit jacket long ago abandoned, showing off her slim figure in her prim white dress shirt and black skirt.

"I don't know how to start this conversation," Samantha said as she walked over to one of the chairs situated in front of his desk, seating herself in his line of sight. "But you seem very different since you came back, Dominic. Did something happen on your trip?"

"I – no, of course not," Dominic said slowly, wondering if he was truly that transparent. Of course something had happened, something that had upended his entire world. But she was gone now and he was being forced back into a world he wasn't so sure he wanted to be in. It was the first time in his entire career he questioned his every step, looking at work as a means to exist instead of something he enjoyed. Samantha regarded him for a moment, her blue eyes showing a hint of sadness in their depths. "I'm just trying to get back into the swing of things, Sam."

"I wish you wouldn't lie to me," she said softly. "I've known you for a long time, Dom. I think I know when you are lying to me or not. Just tell me, what is going on?"

"I don't think I want to do this anymore." The words just rushed out, surprising them both. "I learned something about myself, Sam, and I'm not sure if this life, this job is what I want anymore."

"This job or me?" she asked.

"Both," he answered with some regret, finding it hard to say that one singular word. Sam was his comfort level, his future if he wanted to continue down this career path and become owner. But his plans for the future had changed recently and he wanted to experience life with another woman, a woman he was finding hard to live without. "I'm sorry, Sam."

"Don't be," she said, taking in a breath. Instead of tears, he saw acceptance, respect, and a hint of understanding. "You might find this funny but I'm a bit relieved actually. I love you, Dom, I really do but lately I've questioned the real reason we are getting married. I feel like we are missing out on something, you know? I'm not so sure I want to get married and commit to a long future without it."

"Boy, I'm glad to hear you say that," he said, releasing a shaky breath. He had imagined this scenario a million times in his head and this one he hadn't bet on.

She smiled and reached over the desk, taking his hand in hers. "I'm not sure what's going on in your life, Dom, but all I want is for you to be happy."

"Ditto," Dominic smiled, squeezing her hand lightly. "I didn't mean for this to happen, I really didn't."

"We never do," Samantha said, squeezing his hand back. "But I'm sure you know this means your career at Hamilton is over. I can get Daddy to agree on a great deal of things, but he isn't going to take you breaking my heart lightly no matter what I say."

"Yeah, I know," Dominic swallowed, looking around the office that had been his pride and joy for much of his adult life. He would be giving all of this up on a whim, not sure if Margaret would even take him back after the pain he caused her. He could be out a job and a future with the woman he loved.

"Is she worth it?"

Dominic looked back sharply at Samantha, who had a knowing smile on her face. "I'm not stupid, Dom. You haven't touched me since you came back. I've made my own conclusions. So, is she worth it?"

Dominic took in a deep breath, feeling the hurt, the need to be in Margaret's life, however she would have him. She had consumed his every thought, every fiber of his being since he had returned and somehow Dominic knew he wasn't going to be able to live without her. "Yeah," he finally said, looking into Samantha's eyes, his course set on what he needed to do next. "She's worth it all."

Chapter 23

A week later

"Margaret! Come on girl, snap out of it! We got tables full of customers waiting."

"Sorry, Sharon," Margaret said sheepishly, hefting her tray full of drinks on her hand. "I must have been daydreaming."

"Now's not the time, girlfriend," Sharon said, her eyes full of worry for her friend. "Hey, you okay?"

"Yeah," Margaret said, putting on a forced smile. "I'm good, I'm just tired." Exhausted was more like it for she hadn't slept well at all since returning from the cruise. Nights were the worst, when the memories of Dominic assaulted her, the pain of his betrayal still fresh in her bruised and battered heart. She hated the fact that she had fallen for him so hard, so completely while all the time his heart was tangled with another, his future with someone else that was very different from Margaret.

Despite the torture it caused, Margaret had researched Dominic's life on the internet one night, finding out that her blue-eyed CEO was a big deal, just as the article had alluded. Marrying the owner's daughter would solidify his future and Margaret's heart broke all over again as she realized that even if he hadn't been engaged, she would have never fit into his world. She was just an ordinary waitress.

With a sigh, Margaret set her drinks down at her table, passing them out with her forced smile. This was her life now and it would be best to forget everything that happened on that cruise, including Dominic himself.

"You got another one at section four," Sharon said as she passed by with a tray full of dirty dishes.

"Thanks," Margaret said, picking up her notepad. Turning toward the table, Margaret stopped in her tracks. Now her mind was playing tricks on her. The man in the booth looked suspiciously like the man that invaded her dreams, dressed down in a T-shirt and jeans, his eyes looking away from her as he perused the menu. For a moment the activity stopped around her, her heart banging loudly in her chest. Dominic was here, in her diner, where it all started. A thousand questions ran through her mind as she stared at him, not sure whether she should turn away and leave or run to him. Torn between her heart and her conscience, Margaret decided that she had to get rid of this part of her life once and for all. If she didn't she wouldn't be able to move on past this heartache. Stalking toward the booth, she snatched the menu off the table. "Get out."

Dominic looked up at her and she tried not to melt into those blue eyes, giving him her best pissed-off face. Inside she was dying, but he would never know. "Margaret."

"I said get out," she hissed, pointing to the door. "We don't serve liars here." Oh God he looked ten times better than she had dreamed. He stood then, his eyes searching hers. She saw a myriad of emotions in his depths and steeled against whatever he was going to say. She wouldn't fall for it again. To her surprise, he pulled out a folded-up piece of paper, holding it in his hand.

"I'm sorry," he started. "I'm so damned sorry I didn't tell you about my engagement. I was scared, Margaret. Samantha was the future I had always wanted."

"Are you doing this to torture me?" she said quietly, biting her lip. "Go home, Dominic, go get married."

"You see, that's a problem now," Dominic said sullenly, looking forlorn. "I'm no longer engaged. She wasn't the woman I thought I wanted." He then gave her a small smile, that annoyingly sexy dimple taking her breath away. "You see, there was this woman who spilled a drink on me, invaded my life, and subsequently turned it on its head. She stole my heart and showed me what I had thought was my perfect life was a complete fabrication. Because of her I wasn't happy in my old life. Because of her I lost my job and sold everything off to move to Florida to find that one happiness and hold onto it for dear life."

Margaret sniffed as the first tear fell, warning lights going off in her head at his words. "You quit your job? But, that's your life, Dominic! Why would you do something so stupid?"

"I didn't quit," he said softly, stroking her cheek with his fingers. "I got fired after I broke off my engagement with Samantha. Seems her father didn't enjoy the fact that I wasn't going to be his son-in-law."

"You must go back," she said, her voice trembling now. "This between us is a passing fancy, Dominic. You will regret all of your rash decisions based on lust."

"This is not lust and you know it," Dominic said fiercely, pulling her against him. "I love you, Margaret. I love the fact that you work in this diner but your true passion is dancing. I love the way you make me do things I am totally uncomfortable with. I love the fact you enjoy every little thing in your life and I hope that I can be one of those things."

"Oh, Dominic," Margaret breathed, the tears falling in earnest. This had to be a dream, this man professing his love for her, upending his life to be with her. "We can't, we don't belong together." It was hard for her to say the words, but it was true. He deserved to enjoy what he had worked so hard for, not to give it up for her.

"Please tell me I'm not too late," he said, ignoring her words, his arms tightening around her. "Please tell me you still have faith in us."

"You better say yes or I am going to," Sharon announced beside her. Margaret looked around the diner and noticed everyone was watching them, some of the women dabbing at their eyes with the paper napkins. "Go on, we are all waiting. This is better than any soap opera."

"What do you say, Margaret?" Dominic asked, forcing her to meet his eyes. He was determined, much like she had seen him on the cover of that stupid magazine. He really wanted to be with just her, not making the million-dollar deals she had read about or accomplishing what had been his dreams. He was giving up all of that for her. The thought was overwhelming, the idea that a man like Dominic could love a woman like her, a woman who waited tables for a living. It tugged at her heartstrings. "I love you," he said again, kissing her nose.

"Are you sure?" she asked hesitantly, looking into those eyes she knew so well. God help her, she wanted to live this out for as long as possible.

"I'm sure the thought of what the hell am I doing will cross my mind a time or two," he chuckled. "But then I will lean over and kiss you and forget about the life before you, Margaret. That I am sure of."

"God help us," she said, giving him a wobbly smile. "I love you too so very much."

"Thank God," Dominic breathed, crushing her against him. Applause broke out all around them as he kissed her gently, then dipped her to kiss her again, causing the place to erupt.

"Alright! Alright! That's enough!" Jeff said loudly, though he had a large smile on his face as well. "Everyone back to work! Margaret, take the rest of the night. I'm sure you have more pressing matters to attend to."

"Thank you, Jeff," Margaret said as Dominic grabbed her hand. Jeff winked at her and she let Dominic lead her out into the sunshine, where he pulled her close again, pressing the paper into her hand. "Open it."

Puzzled, Margaret opened the folded paper and looked at the address. "Okay, so is this your new house or something?"

"Better," he grinned, pushing her toward a sporty-looking car. "I need to show you something."

"I see you can't take the CEO out of you completely," she said dryly as she climbed into the posh leather interior.

"Well, I sold off everything else," Dominic said as he climbed in and threw the shifter into drive. "There was no way I was going to sell this car."

Margaret laughed as they started down the road, her hand firmly in his. She couldn't believe it. Dominic was here, at her side and she could keep him for as long as she wanted to. They were together, just as she had imagined. He had given everything up for her and there was no way she was going to ever let him go. After about five minutes of driving, he pulled up at a small building in a busy part of town, kissing her hand before opening the door. "Come on."

Her curiosity getting the better of her, Margaret climbed out and walked hand in hand with Dominic to the front door, surprised when he pulled out a set of keys. "This, madam, is your new dance studio," he said, pushing the door open with a flourish. Margaret walked into the space, taking note of the openness of the front room, a perfect place to install dance bars and hold classes. "It needs some work but I think we can make it work," Dominic was saying as he crossed the space. "There's an upstairs where I will run my investment business. You can have the entire downstairs for your studio, Margaret."

"Y-you bought this?" Margaret stammered, overwhelmed with love for this man.

"I did and it was hard to do without you," he said, his hands in his pockets. "If you don't like it, we can look at other places. The real estate agent assured me you would have great traffic here. I got it at a decent price. I think I won her over with my good looks."

Margaret ran to him and flung her arms around his neck, kissing him hard. "I can't, this is, I love the heck out of you."

"Well," Dominic laughed, spinning her around. "I wonder what I would get if I bought you a three-story building." Margaret laughed then, her heart nearly bursting with joy. In a million years she couldn't imagine that she would be this happy, that her life would take such a roller coaster ride and still end up perfect. "I love you, Margaret."

Kissing him softly, Margaret gave him a saucy smile, running her fingers over the skin just above his T-shirt. "You know, this building is missing one thing."

"What's that?" Dominic asked, his brows coming together in a frown. "I'm sure I measured it correctly compared to the one you currently use."

"It's missing some lovemaking," she whispered into his ear, nuzzling his neck. "I believe this building adventure should start off on the right foot."

"I like the way you think," he said wolfishly, laughing as he picked her up in his arms, striding to the stairs. "We will start in my office to ward off bad karma."

What to read next?

If you liked this book, you will also like *The Weekend Girlfriend*. Another interesting book is *Two Reasons to Be Single*.

The Weekend Girlfriend

Jessica has worked hard to be the paralegal that hotshot, sexy attorney Kyle needs. Unfortunately he doesn't see her as just his paralegal but also his own personal assistant. When he blames her for a mix-up in his personal life, Jessica sees no other option but to quit, thinking that her time with him is over. Much to her surprise, Kyle makes a proposition to her that she never thought she would hear coming from his lips. He needs a temporary girlfriend for his sister's wedding and he wants her to be that person. Jessica accepts the challenge and finds herself thrown into his world, learning things about him she never knew. The more time she spends with him outside of work, the more she is drawn to Kyle. As the wedding draws near, she finds herself fighting off some strong feelings for the man. When the wedding weekend is over, will Jessica be able to walk away from Kyle with her heart intact?

Two Reasons to Be Single

Olivia Parker has a job doing what she loves, a wonderful family and plenty of friends, but no luck in the love department. Tired of worrying about it, she decides to swear off love completely and focus on all the good things in her life. Just as she makes her firm resolution, Jake Harper arrives in town and knocks her plans into a tailspin. As the excited single ladies of Morning Glory surround the extremely attractive newcomer, Olivia steers clear of the "casserole brigade," as she calls the women, and tries to keep her distance from Jake. Instead, a variety of situations throw them together and they get to know each other better. They both have reasons for not wanting to get involved in a relationship, but the chemistry between them ignites, even as they desperately attempt to keep it at bay. As things heat up between Olivia and Jake, there is an aura of mystery about him that leaves Olivia certain that he is hiding something. When Jake disappears for a few days without telling Olivia that he is going out of town, she hates the way it makes her feel, and it reminds her of why she was giving up on dating in the first place. As Olivia's feelings for Jake grow, so does the need to find out what exactly brought him to Morning Glory and what he's been hiding.

About Emily Walters

Emily Walters lives in California with her beloved husband, three daughters, and two dogs. She began writing after high school, but it took her ten long years of writing for newspapers and magazines until she realized that fiction is her real passion. Emily likes to create a mental movie in her reader's mind about charismatic characters, their passionate relationships and interesting adventures. When she isn't writing romantic stories, she can be found reading a fiction book, jogging, or traveling with her family. She loves Starbucks, Matt Damon and Argentinian tango.

One Last Thing…

If you believe that *Cruising for Love* is worth sharing, would you spend a minute to let your friends know about it?

If this book lets them have a great time, they will be enormously grateful to you – as will I.

Emily

www.EmilyWaltersBooks.com